CROSSING THE ROAD

OTHER INDIAINK TITLES

Anjana Basu	*Black Tongue*
A.N.D. Haksar	*Madhav & Kama: A Love Story from Ancient India*
Boman Desai	*Servant, Master, Mistress*
C.P. Surendran	*An Iron Harvest*
Chitra Banerjee Divakaruni	*The Mirror of Fire and Dreaming*
I. Allan Sealy	*The Everest Hotel*
I. Allan Sealy	*Trotternama*
Indrajit Hazra	*The Garden of Earthly Delights*
Jaspreet Singh	*17 Tomatoes: Tales from Kashmir*
Jawahara Saidullah	*The Burden of Foreknowledge*
Kalpana Swaminathan	*The Page 3 Murders*
Kalpana Swaminathan	*The Gardener's Song*
Kamalini Sengupta	*The Top of the Raintree*
Madhavan Kutty	*The Village Before Time*
Pankaj Mishra	*The Romantics*
Paro Anand	*I'm Not Butter Chicken*
Paro Anand	*Wingless*
Ramchandra Gandhi	*Muniya's Light: A Narrative of Truth and Myth*
Ranjit Lal	*The Life &Times of Altu-Faltu*
Ranjit Lal	*The Small Tigers of Shergarh*
Rashme Sehgal	*Hacks and Headlines*
Raza Mir & Ali Husain Mir	*Anthems of Resistance: A Celebration of Progressive Urdu Poetry*
Sanjay Bahadur	*The Sound of Water*
Shandana Minhas	*Tunnel Vision*
Selina Sen	*A Mirror Greens in Spring*
Sharmistha Mohanty	*New Life*
Shree Ghatage	*Brahma's Dream*
Susan Visvanathan	*Something Barely Remembered*
Susan Visvanathan	*The Visiting Moon*
Susan Visvanathan	*The Seine at Noon*
Tom Alter	*The Longest Race*

FORTHCOMING TITLES

John McLithon	*Hindutva, Sex and Adventure*
Tushar Raheja	*Run Romi Run*

SUDHIR THAPLIYAL

CROSSING THE ROAD

IndiaInk
ROLI BOOKS

First published in India in 2009
IndiaInk
An imprint of
Roli Books Pvt. Ltd.
M-75, G.K. II Market, New Delhi 110 048
Phone: +91 (011) 40682000
Fax: +91 (011) 2921 7185
E-mail: info@rolibooks.com
Website: www.rolibooks.com
Also at Bangalore, Chennai, Jaipur, Kolkata,
Mumbai & Varanasi

Design: Supriya Saran

ISBN: 978-81-86939-48-2

Typeset in Trump Mediaeval by Roli Books Pvt. Ltd.
and printed at Anubha Printers, Noida

For
Nisha and Tushna

Dedicated to
the memory of
Biri, Kinny and Yogi. Friends.

PROLOGUE

'O Hamlet, what a falling off was there . . .'
Shakespeare

Near the mausoleum of Nizamuddin Chisti, in the city of ghosts and djinns, ruined forts and palaces, massacres and assassinations, whores and saints, battlefields and mass graves a tall, emaciated and dark man with long, unkempt hair and a beard and dressed in a black kaftan, that has not been washed in years, can be seen circling the tomb from time to time. He ends each round by crossing the busy road at a rapid pace, mindless and heedless of the traffic that zips past him at a terrifying speed. Neither does he look left, nor does he look right. Cars, buses and trucks sail past him without a stop. He then does the return journey in a similar fashion and begins his perambulation again.

Several of the beggars who hang around on the pavement that runs along the site of this well-worshipped shrine have been watching this impassively for years. No one knows or cares who this man is and, in the fitness of things mystical, no one wants to question his existence. But he is there all right and if you know English you can hear him muttering through clenched teeth – 'come alive, come alive' – as he circles the great Sufi saint's mortal remains.

And on the days when Sufi singers gather near the spot the man can be seen very much like a heron standing on one leg, with his eyes closed and head cocked slightly towards the music, listening to the ghazals.

He's simply called the man who crosses the road. But I know who he is because I put him there. It is the hell his mortal soul has been assigned to.

Midway upon the journey of our life
I found myself within a forest dark,
For the straightforward pathway had been lost.

Dante Alighieri

'Children! When crossing the road, first look right and then left.'

Those who have grown up in the hills and forests, like me and several other wise men, know there are only two ways to go anywhere. Your destination can be up the hill or down the hill. There are no left and no right turns. Even when you come to a fork in the road you either go down or up. Somewhat similar to what happens to people who have to use lifts or elevators, as they call them in the U.S. of A. There is nothing like taking a wrong turn. And you don't have to look left or right when crossing the hallway because there is no traffic to worry about.

When life is made so simple for you from the day you learn to walk you grow up into a cheerful and carefree individual and not necessarily mentally challenged. You don't need to learn the difficult art of taking decisions. Life becomes an uncomplicated business and you trudge along merrily up and down the hills and dales with not a worry in the world and not a paisa in your pocket.

Nearly all the people who live in the plains cannot understand this individual from the hills. They, the plains people, spend all their life making wrong turns and landing up in all kinds of trouble. They find complications in the simplest of matters and indecision and bad decisions mark their existence on this earth and sometimes even after they are dead and gone. Their gods are increasingly complex and difficult to appease and that is an indication of why they are different from the gods in the hills who either bestow favours or don't. Like good old Shiva! The only member of the Trinity who has no Papa and no Mama.

However, in the hills, Nature conspires against people in myriad ways. Landslides, avalanches, extreme cold, droughts, iodine deprivation, malnutrition and earthquakes make these areas really inhospitable. But people continue to live there when if they had lived in the plains, Shiva forbid, they would have only to face the odd flood or epidemic or war. This necessary stubbornness is rooted again in the rather simple desire to live a life where there are no left and no right turns. Here 'simple', unlike Simple Simon, is not a mentally retarded person.

So, one fine summer morning as I basked under the dappled shade of the plum tree in my little garden that overlooks the biggest valley in India, I was rather taken aback by my friend Menon's remark. He said he wished he could live the way I lived. Menon is from the deep South – from a countryside rich with paddy and the fragrance of a thousand spices and dotted with palms and coconuts, clear lagoons, beaches and the sea and a monsoon that rarely fails the people. And also writers, artists and dancers with big bosoms and bigger buttocks.

A land of plenty and above average IQs because there is plenty of iodine as opposed to folks in the hills who suffer from iodine deficiency and consequent low IQs, according to Menon. In short, he thinks most hill people are duffers. He says he is from God's own country and hill folk maintain they live in the Land of the Gods – Devlok. They never mention the fact that their temples have been robbed of their idols by thieves from the plains. This difference in attitudes may be explained by the different altitudes! Here you have one lot down at mean sea level and the other up on the snowline or as near to it to sustain life. But that is neither here nor there as far as this story goes.

Menon is a man of many parts but on that day he was a tired advertising executive 're-charging his batteries', as he put it, with a quick holiday in my cottage in the hills. At the back of my cottage where a dirt track brought visitors to the main house was a little space where he had parked his spanking new Mercedes. Alongside was a Honda City that belonged to his ex-wife.

I have often been asked why I have friends who keep coming for holidays and who bring their ex-wives or some girlfriend or the other but never their wives. Maybe, and then maybe not, they don't trust a crusty old divorcee alone with their wives. I have no real answer to that question except to mouth the old cliché 'different strokes for different people' or some such inanity. Most often than not they quarrel bitterly after a few drinks and expletives flow thick and fast with vile accusations of all kinds. Lover's quarrels, I'm told but I have reservations on that.

Since nearly all the visitors to my house are from the plains and are friends I made when I lived in the 'big city' where I made several wrong turns and bad decisions, I can understand their irrevocable need to be confused. They like to torture themselves by being convinced that they are born losers and that life has been one hell of a drudge. Their children have all grown up either into paragons of youth or are absolute write-offs who need to be detoxed on a regular basis. Their bank balances bloated to bursting could be fatter. Their wives have become plain and fat pains and vice versa. I have women friends too, you should know.

So, Menon on that summer morning mourned the absence of happiness in his life. I listened to him as I usually do because I know that these friends of mine, generally speaking, come to sound off about their problems at home and at work. I nod sympathetically and make odd noises to reinforce my sympathy and from time to time make sure that his glass is full of the poison of the day. Overhead, a flight of parrots whooshes past and the neighbourhood pair of kestrels circle endlessly in the blue sky.

Menon was talking about infidelities, of and by his wife, office colleagues, his motor mechanic, electrician, plumber and most of the people he had to cohabit with while he made a walloping packet. If I hadn't known Menon I would have said the man was a whinger. But I knew him. If at all he had something to say it would be nonsense, something out of Alice in Wonderland. He practiced a sense of a wry humour, specially when he talked about domestics. Proud of his feudal background, he usually made strenuous efforts to be nice to the help. But they saw through his condescensions. And he knew that.

Menon had made his first million when he was an aspiring advertising account executive and there were many stories making the rounds on how he had gone about doing that. In Bombay, before it became Mumbai, cocktails, most of the talk revolved around who was screwing whom in bed and out of it. Known to be a successful womanizer, Menon had no qualms about doing it. He often claimed he had screwed every female who ever came within striking distance in or out of office. It was up to the listener to believe him. I took many of his stories with large dollops of salt. Not that it made any difference to him. Ditto for his financial conquests.

Life had been good to him, the by-pass surgeries and stents notwithstanding. His ex-wife was in the bath preening herself before she came and joined us for her elevenses. I had made her potion of vodka, lemon juice and green chillies and it was in a jug full of ice. She had, she claimed, learnt this cocktail from some maharani or the other and it was a surefire cure for any kind of a hangover. I believed her because if anyone knew about her hangovers and the kind of foul mood she was in the mornings he or she would have the concoction standing by the moment she surfaced.

She was Leela. Had at one time been Leela Patronobis, then Leela Patwardhan and was currently Leela Menon looking for another husband. When she was in a good mood, and that was only after she had had two drinks of her potion, she would tell all and sundry that her full name was Leela Patronobis Patwardhan Menon. Her much-divorced lifestyle and a generally degenerate drinking and eating fetish had, surprisingly, not left many scars on her physical appearance. She had swung through her two pregnancies and had gone through her menopause without a whistle stop. Now in her mid-fifties she still had a youthful figure and a spring in her walk.

On that morning, she had put on a lemon chiffon sari and

a backless blouse held up by spaghetti straps. Her breasts were firm and rounded and she did not need a bra to keep them high and pointed. Her stomach was flat and her arse tight. Menon had hinted at a visit to Silicon California, not to be confused with Silicon Valley, where she had got an implant and a chin tuck in. But to an untrained observer like me she was a juicy bit of crumpet and I wouldn't have minded romping around in bed with her. That is, if she would have given me the time of the day. She didn't think much of struggling writers like me though she often softened up and told Menon that I was more handsome than any of her husbands or lovers, but she would be damned if she was going to waste her time with fellows like me who don't have a penny to their name.

In short, she was what are known as gold diggers and the purpose of her visit to my cottage was to make Menon cough up some of his millions for an out-of-court settlement. I knew about that because the night before while she was toying around with the food on her plate she had said in ominous tones – 'Menon, have you thought about it?'

Menon was called Menon by everyone though he did have a first name – Hariharan. Maybe his mother or father called him that but I had never heard anyone call him anything else except his minions who called him Mr Menon. Even his current mistress called him Menon. The only difference was that she would add the obsequious north Indian 'ji' and at times of excessive demands would call him Menon, Sirr! The sir's r rolled like a gargling throat. I once asked him what she called him in bed and he said he didn't remember because by the time he could muster up the desire to bed her he would be drunk as a coot.

Leela walked out of the house and joined us under the plum tree's shade. I placed a glass of vodka with lemon juice and green chillies in front of her. She grabbed it with both hands and as her whole body went into spasms managed to put the glass to her lips and knock down the potion in one go except for a faint trickle down her chin. For a long moment we sat there looking at her as she sat with eyes closed, glass clenched in both hands and then she gave a loud, unladylike burp and banged the glass on the table. 'Pour on McDuff,' she said.

I did my part of the job while her now steady hands managed to light a cigarette that she inserted into a long, black holder. After a long drag she let the smoke out through her nostrils and gave a satisfied sigh as she reached for the second glass of vodka. Menon was watching impassively and he knew from long experience to never intrude in that moment of exquisite, almost divinely spiritual bliss, which Leela enjoyed without recognizing anybody or anything around her. Even my Doggie had learnt to stay away from her till she broke the silence, as it were.

Then she said, 'Good morning, all.'

'Good morning,' we chorused.

'You know I had a dream last night,' she said.

'Not again!' said Menon.

'Yes, Moron Menon. People dream, you know.'

'Oops! Didn't know,' Moron Menon said and grimaced.

'Balls-all-you-know, you cunning Tamil bastard,' Leela the Punjabi harridan said.

'Hey. Take it easy. It's only eleven in the morning,' I said. 'And he's not Tamil.'

'Shut up!' Leela told me.

I took another sip of my drink and Menon did the same. A pleasant breeze drifted up the hillside and my lawn was filled with the sweet smell of ripening fruits in the orchard. A family of Seven Sisters emerged from under the hydrangea and seeing us darted off. Doggie gave them a brief chase and came back and parked himself at Leela's feet where she kicked him in the ribs. She was like that. If he had nipped her dainty ankles she would have been all over him, caressing him and making lovey doggie noises.

'Well, I slept with god last night,' she began again.

'You did not, you lying bitch,' Menon said.

'I dreamt that, you arsehole,' she said.

'What happened then?' I asked hoping to keep the peace.

'You see how nice this man is, Moron Menon. He cares. He wants to listen to me.'

'I bet he does. After all he makes a living out of writing what other people say,' Menon replied tartly.

'I don't care. Anyway, the dream goes like this. I am

standing before god along with two other women. He wants to know what we've been up to in our lives on earth. The first woman, she was ugly, says, "I prayed and fasted, my lord". Send her to heaven, ordered god. The second woman, she was obese, said she enjoyed gossiping, drinking and eating. God said, "Send her to hell". Then it was my turn. I told him I had spent a life of pleasure, vicarious pleasure, made love to all your creatures, men and women, doggies and horses, drank myself silly every day and want to do it all over again. God pondered on that and then ordered that I be sent to his bedroom.' She laughed raucously.

That was the signal for us to know that she was back in a good mood, her heebie-jeebies well taken care of, and we could hope for some more pleasant times so long as the booze kept flowing. So, we made the obligatory smiles.

Leela's hallucinations were known and subject of much gossip from one end of the country's cocktail circuit to the other. They ranged from fantasies that defied imagination, to ghosts male and female, spiders of all colours and plants that were hell bent on eating her. She particularly disliked a blood red geranium that nestled in a pot on my windowsill. She had made a number of attempts to destroy the plant but had been caught in the act before she could do much damage. When asked why she wanted to destroy a harmless flower she said it frightened her. So, my servant of many winters removed the flowerpot and put it away far from her itching fingers.

Punditji, as the serving man was called, had seen so many of these hysterical females all over the hills that he had lost count. He often asked me why I put myself through the unnecessary torture of hosting these people and I always told him I didn't know. Maybe I felt sorry for them. At times I thought I could help them out of their miserable existence. But none of these were convincing arguments. In the hills, women long denied a healthy sex life because their husbands were away working in the plains or serving in the army, find some form of release by throwing violent bouts of hysteria. Since people don't know better they claim the woman has been possessed either by a goddess or a fiendish spirit. There are many ways of calming her down. In milder cases the Gayatri mantra does the trick. But in more severe ones a specialist is called in, who thrashes her with a broom till the evil spirit runs for his or her life. But Sigmund Freud changed all that when he described something called uterine hysteria which he said affected the female when she wasn't being satisfied, to put it unscientifically.

Leela's hysterics were of another kind and Punditji was of the opinion that a simple mantra won't help. What she needed, he said, was severe flogging with a whip made of leaves of the stinging nettle. I told him to keep his antidotes to himself and fished around for some Valium in my medicine box. That would help but then Leela would get maudlin which was not so interesting. Menon, who had been told about Punditji's idea, said it was worth a try because if nothing else the bitch deserved a whipping. He was also into sado-masochism.

Both of them had, on that particular visit, been in my cottage for almost a week and not a single day had passed when there weren't severe outbreaks of hysteria, temper tantrums and long bursts of invectives and expletives. But what eventually got my goat was Leela's habit of throwing crockery around and kicking my doggie whenever and wherever. This I particularly resented.

One day she took off all her clothes and began dancing on the lawn. It was a sort of rain dance because that afternoon there had been a violent thunderstorm and heavy hail and rain. As the song goes '. . . along with sunshine there's got to be some rain . . . ' Just then the postman walked in with my mail and I knew that by the evening the whole town would know about Leela's antics. The poor man had unfurled his umbrella because of the rain and now he covered his face with it to save himself the embarrassment of seeing a naked, gyrating Leela. Moron Menon sat under the plum tree, a wide grin on his face and enjoyed the spectacle. I hustled the postman away saying that the memsahib was offering a special prayer for it to rain in the plains where there had been a delayed monsoon. The poor man nodded in understanding. Possibly he had heard of the rites in parts of the country where peasant women danced naked in their fields to appease the rain god.

Punditji had been watching all this from his kitchen window and wasn't too pleased with the goings on. I had retreated into the glazed verandah and gazed at the not so unpleasant spectacle on my lawn. She did have a superb figure and she could dance very well. Her breasts jiggled and heaved with every twist of her torso and her bare buttocks swung to a rhythm of their own. Raindrops splashed her and ran down in small rivulets finding every crevice and crack in her body. As someone said, it was a sight fit for the gods.

But apparently the gods thought otherwise. There was a big burst of lightning followed by a thunderclap and Leela was brought to the ground either by the blast or the shock. She jerked once or twice and then lay very still. I ran out to see what had happened. Punditji too ran out with a blanket and we wrapped her in it. The rain had stopped as suddenly as it had come and I scooped her in my arms and brought her indoors. Menon had managed to hobble inside and the first thing he wanted to know was if the bitch was dead.

'Not yet,' I told him as I rubbed her wet hair with a towel.

He didn't believe me and started feeling for a pulse.

'Shit! She's alive!' he exclaimed.

'It will take many a thunderstorm to kill Leela,' I told him.

Punditji was rubbing the soles of her feet and the massage seemed to help because she opened her eyes and after staring blankly at us vomited. Out came the vodka, lemon juice and chillies and made a nasty mess on the blanket. I picked her up again and took her to her room where I laid her out on the bed, threw the blanket into the bathroom and covered her up in a thick quilt. I left her there and went to ring for the doctor because I didn't know how to treat people suffering from shock. On the other end of the line, the phone system had miraculously escaped being damaged, Doc Rawat told me not to worry and asked me to give her a glass of warm milk with lots of sugar. He said he would drop in later in the day.

When I told Menon what the doctor had prescribed for her, he chuckled.

'Milk,' he said, 'will be the death of her. Get it fast and stuff it down her throat while she's still not conscious.'

He chuckled some more and went off to pour himself a drink at the sideboard.

After an hour or so we heard moans and groans coming from her room and in a feeble voice she asked for Menon.

'Your spouse calls,' I informed him.

'Ex-spouse, you silly bugger,' he said and shakily made his way to her room.

What happened in there would remain one of the greatest mysteries that I have encountered. At that point in time I had no idea what Menon saw when he went into the room. All I can say is that when he came out he was walking open-mouthed, eyes open but not seeing, bumping into the furniture and making gasping sounds. For a second I thought he was having a heart attack and rushed to help him to a chair. I sat him down and he just sprawled out, his body limp and except for his laboured breathing he might as well have been dead.

'Looks like he's finished,' Punditji said in a solemn voice reserved for the lately departed.

'I don't think so,' I said and proceeded to give him a heart massage as I had seen people doing on television. The problem with practicing what one has seen on television is that it never seems to work. At any rate it doesn't work as fast as it does on the idiot box. Menon had gone comatose, a sight I had seen many times with a lot of drunks and I was tempted to leave him alone and let him come out of his stupor in due time. At any rate, I slipped off his moccasins and with Punditji's help laid him out on the settee.

We threw a blanket over him and moved back to the lawn to enjoy the sun that had emerged from the bank of dark clouds that were now racing away towards the southern horizon. Over the blue hills in the east a double rainbow arched its way through the sky and possibly there was a pot of gold at the end of the rainbow that disappeared into the Ganga valley.

When Doc Rawat rang the doorbell I was much relieved. I now had two palpably sick people and didn't know what to do with them. I would hate them to die in my house not because their death would make any difference to my life but because of the complications that would follow. Like informing the police, postmortems and arranging for their bodies to be shipped back to wherever they had come from and so on and so forth. And, furthermore, all kinds of explanations to the kith and kin on their bereavement.

The doctor is another mountain man like me. He knows his medicine and knows how to keep complications out of his life.

'What's up?' he asked me.

'I've got two patients for you. One is traumatized by lightning and the other by seeing some kind of an apparition, I think,' I told him.

'Must be the booze. Really, your friends drink too much and I think you, too. Take it easy, will you, and save me a lot of grief,' he said.

Since Menon was stretched out on the settee and was on the way to Leela's room the doctor examined him first. He felt his pulse, poked around with his stethoscope and took his blood pressure.

'Just as I thought. He's plain drunk. Blood pressure is on the high side but that is to be expected with his obesity and the amount he drinks. Let him sleep it off. He'll be fine when he wakes up,' he diagnosed and asked me to take him to Leela's room.

We walked into her room to find her sleeping. I watched from the door and except for the low moans from time to time she looked very much like a sleeping doll. The doctor went through his routine.

'The pulse is a bit weak but she's strong as a horse and should come out of this soon. Give her a lot of fluids but no alcohol for the next twenty-four hours. She's dehydrated,' he explained.

We left her room and moved to the sideboard where I poured the doctor a whisky that he swallowed in one shot.

'Where do you find such friends?' he wanted to know.

'Here and there,' I said.

'Oh! Well, better luck next time,' he said and left.

I pondered his parting words and restless after the afternoon's proceedings called for Doggie and went for a stroll. The storm had dumped broken twigs, leaves and ripening fruit all over. The smell of wet earth gave me a big charge of energy and with great vigour I stepped onto the path that leaves my house to meet up with the main road.

As we walked along I wondered what made people like Menon and Leela tick. I mean did they wonder about characters like me. Reclusive, drifting with the tide, least inclined to buck the system. Or did they think that writers and painters were just layabouts who needed to be tolerated because they had some conversational value. Nearly everyone I know in the world of the fine arts, except for one or two people, is perpetually broke. That is not saying too much. It is a simple observation and best left for others to be judgemental about.

But to get back to my houseguests and, in this case, Menon and Leela. The doctor had by dismissing them as drunks taken a major burden away from my over imaginative mind. Now I did not need to think about morbid things like cadavers and their removal and all that needless trouble that people take with dead humans. The pure air and walk had cleaned the cobwebs formed in my head by excessive booze and when I returned I was ready to take on another round of hard drinking.

Menon was lying as I had left him with his eyes closed but his ears seemed to be alive because he asked if it was me. Hearing him raised my spirits a few notches more and I asked him if he was feeling better.

'Like death warmed over,' he mumbled and made a sign with his hand. It was the signal for a drink.

He trembled violently, more like spasms. Then he let out his breath with a loud whoosh and turned on his side, his knees tucked into his stomach. The blanket had slipped and I spread it on him evenly. Menon was one lame duck, I told myself.

Then I took a peep into Leela's room. She was fast asleep and her bosom moved gently under the quilt. I left her to her dreams and wondered what kind of god had dispatched her to his bedroom and what had come of that encounter. I smiled to myself when I remembered her descriptions of various men who had floundered in bed with her unable to cope with her sexual demands and aggression. 'Sucked the bastard dry', was her favourite description for most of her lovers. I suddenly felt sorry for that particular god in her dream.

Punditji cornered me near the bar and wanted to know what to cook for dinner. I asked him to keep it light and a kedgeree with curd would do very well for all of us. It is the kind of food given to sick people and who was to say we were not sick physically and, possibly, mentally. I knew we were definitely not run of the mill people. I mean folks like farmers, coolies, clerks, shopkeepers and other working stiffs like them who lived as multiple personalities keeping one face for people they met in public and another for the ones they knew in private and yet another for the ones they met in dark recesses and dirty back rooms.

I secretly prided myself on my lifestyle as I didn't have to account for it to anyone except my liver. The same for people like Leela and Menon. They didn't have to be middle-class hypocrites. They were rich and that combined with a disdain for most moral values made them what they were.

In a manner of speaking you could defend them and say that they lived truthful lives because human beings consider truth a great virtue. Our national motto says 'Truth will be Victorious', whatever that means. And the Americans trust in god, whoever that entity is. The French have possibly got it right with liberty, equality and fraternity. What about Eskimos or pygmies or the Jarawas of the Andamans? Surely they must have a god and if they don't, how come Christian missionaries missed out on a lot of them? They got the naked natives in the Amazon, Dark Africa, the jungles of the northeast of India and several such unheard of and unlivable places and managed to convince them that the Christian God was the 'bestest'.

Bestest, was Leela's favourite word. She used it without a care for grammatical niceties, the English language for you or me who like to believe that they know the patois of an island people who once believed that the sun never set on their empire. Leela used to maintain that 'sin' never set on the Raj. It was the day after the lightning strike and she had joined me at my favourite spot under the plum tree for an unheard cup of tea. As far as I knew, her mornings started with a vodka pick-me-up and a prolonged session before the mirror in what was known to all who knew her as a face makeover.

That morning I saw her for the first time without a shadow of make-up. She was fair-skinned or what the marriage ads described as 'wheatish complexion'. The ravages of time had turned her laugh lines into wrinkles and her upper lip without the usual gloss had vertical cracks or fine fissures, if that is an apt description. The dappled shade of the plum tree did manage to mask her face from time to time as a slight breeze shook the leaves. Dark shadows under her eyes, almost like black eyes some men give to their women who then flaunt them around as a sign of the magnificent love their men have for them, looked like grotesque dark glasses that had slipped off her light brown eyes. She hadn't said a word since the last afternoon. Now noticing my scrutiny of her features she pulled the dressing gown tight around her neck and crossed her arms over her breasts.

'Tea?' I asked incredulously.

'Is something wrong with your ears? You curious, always-wanting-to-know, busybody. I want tea,' she said in her gravelly voice. 'And don't be chintzy,' she added for good effect.

I poured her a cup and asked if she would like it with sugar and milk. She grunted which could have meant anything so I went through the ritual anyway. She took a sip and spat it out.

'What's this? Dishwater?'

She was edgy and bad tempered and I told her so. It is one thing to be a sympathetic friend and ignore rudeness because of the circumstances. I mean she had just been hit by or nearly hit by lightning, divorced and without a few millions to her name. It is, however, mildly irritating to be sitting on one's own property under one's favourite plum tree, watching the sun rise over the blue hills and being told off by a palpably hung over and rude woman who wasn't even looking beautiful. Strangely enough my ticking her off mellowed her and she said she was sorry. Women like Leela go through life without saying sorry or thank you. And yet they are loved for this rather uncivil mannerism. It's kind of cute, one besotted man had told me once. He was the type who would drink champagne from her sandals.

Before she could say another word I got up and went to fetch her a vodka. That did the trick. She was improving by the second and after a couple of more drinks her face softened and even the harsh lines of dissipation and age seemed to be weaker. Maybe it was the change in the sun's position. She smiled, a fleeting kind of twist to her lips that made men want to be her slaves.

'My! I must be looking a scream. I haven't even got my face on. This isn't the bestest day in my life, is it?' Leela said.

I gave a short laugh that was non-committal. It's a little trick I had picked up over the years when I didn't want to say yes or no. It worked most of the times except on occasions when the person asking a question would ask what I meant by that. In reply I would give him or her the same laugh and leave the rest to their imagination. At any rate, that was enough for Leela to get up and go inside to put on her face, as she described it. She passed Menon on the steps and just cocked her chin. It was neither a nod nor a sign of recognition nor a greeting.

Menon still in his pajamas and dressing gown shuffled over and asked, 'Who was that old hag?'

This time I gave a loud guffaw, loud enough to scare the Seven Sisters into a short flight and make Doggie take notice of his surroundings.

'That was your ex-wife, you drunken sod,' I told him.

'Never,' he said.

Menon had gone into denial which was all for the best because it was still too early in the morning to debate the question.

'Tea?' I asked.

'You mad or something?' said Menon.

Menon could speak idiomatically correct English. When he didn't want to he would lapse into Anglo-Indian where verbs, conjunctions and such other tools of viable communication were thrown to the winds.

'Me? No maddest, you old fart,' I said sticking my chin out. 'You land up here on my doorstep with your old hag of an ex-wife who dances nude on my lawn and thus invites the wrath of the lightning god, whoever he is, to strike us and nearly throw us into space. So, you mad or something?'

Menon scratched his balls rather meditatively. Other men would have done the same thing to their beard or head in public. Or to the back of their head. It is an old ploy to signal that heavy thinking is going on about some matter or the other. The fact is that those who do these antics have switched off their thinking machine. Menon had gone into a world where I didn't exist.

He came out of his reverie and made that curious signal with his hand that was a signal for a drink. I don't know where he had picked it up. Maybe he had attended some course in sign language or lived with people who had not yet invented the spoken word. His right hand would twist clockwise at the wrist once and then return to normal and begin an anti-clockwise movement. I tried to copy him once or twice but it never seemed to work for me.

'Isn't it a bit early?' I said.

'What? Is this the temperance society or AA or what?' Menon asked.

I didn't bother to reply and instead brought him a drink and made one for myself too. What the hell? I told myself. If you can't fight 'em, join 'em, as someone once said.

It was going to be a profound day or a day for profundities, from the looks of it. Punditji asked if anyone was interested in breakfast but Menon waved him away in dismissal. Punditji didn't like that hand signal. So he went inside and brought the bottle of vodka out and thumped it on the table at Menon's side in a gesture of disapproval.

'That's my man,' Menon said and slipped a century into his shirt pocket. That was his way of making up for rudeness to servants.

Inside the house the phone rang and rang till Punditji picked it up. It was for Menon and Punditji handed the cordless phone over to him.

'Hello! Hello!' said Menon. It was his call sign, sort of. On the other end a woman's voice said something.

It's that bloody woman, Menon announced to the world at large and into the phone said, 'Oye beautiful.'

That 'bloody woman' was his current mistress who called him Menonji or Menon sirr, depending on what she wanted from him.

I got away and took a turn around the garden while Menon chatted her up and then with a loud 'shut up!' switched the phone off.

'Same thing. All over again. I tell you, women can't be creative. She goes on and on about matters of no consequence. Who am I sitting with? Why? How much did you have to drink? Makes me feel like I'm some kind of a schoolboy. No?' Menon was fuming.

'I don't know. I don't have bimbos for mistresses. Besides, why do you tolerate her if she is a pain?' I said.

'Kick her out? You mad or something. She'll make my waking life hell. Well, coming to think of it, I could pay her bloody off. How much do you think she'd settle for?'

'How the hell would I know? I've never been able to afford a mistress and the last time I paid for a fuck was when I was a university man,' I told him.

'Come on. You must have an idea. After all you do meet all

kinds. Why don't you ask around and get me a ballpark figure?'

I looked at him wondering where he got his silly ideas. Did he really expect me to ring up so and so or any Tom, Dick and Harry who may or may not have had a mistress. I could run an opinion poll, put an ad in the papers or on television or just sit on a bench on the Mall and quiz passers by. Something like: Say, how do you get rid of a mistress? Suppose someone did not like my line of questioning or the subject matter and decided to punch me in the nose. Then what?

It was like the nursery rhyme: *Here we go around the mulberry bush . . .*

Instead, I told him to get on with the vodka and maybe he will get an idea. That's what he always said when pondering an advertising campaign or a copy. In the past, a number of his office colleagues had told me how Menon would disappear into a nearby bar in search of a slogan, caption or an idea and return a few hours later all charged up with ideas. Some of them did work and that explained his fortune.

While Menon shuffled off to look 'presentable', Leela returned. She had put on fresh make-up, a Spanish blouse with a deep cleavage and toreador pants and stiletto heels. Her hair was freshly combed and she looked her usual sexy self. But I knew better now that I had seen her in the harsh light of the early morning sun without her make-up and without a drink in my stomach. All the same I did feel a twinge in my penis.

She placed the glass of vodka on the table, sat herself down, lit a cigarette, inserted it into her cigarette holder, puffed and exhaled. The ritual over, she uncrossed her legs and leaning her face on her elbows resting on the table she looked at me from a distance of a foot and said, 'I've got an idea.'

I enjoyed the full view of her breasts and without looking her in the eyes said, 'What idea?'

'I know how to screw Moron Menon.'

'So, tell me,' I said and looked her in the eye.

'Promise you won't tell him,' she said.

I made the obligatory sign of a promise and mumbled 'hope to die'.

She thought about something for a while and then in her

usual way told me she didn't trust me. 'Men always bond and stick together,' she observed.

'As you like,' I said and to change the subject said, 'Tell me how you broke the news of wanting to leave Menon.'

'I simply told him I wanted to split.'

'What did he say?'

'He just looked nonplussed.'

'Now where were you two when this conversation took place?'

'In bed, of course. He was waiting for the Viagra to take effect and I was getting bored lying around while he fondled my tits. You must appreciate my timing. The moment I felt a stirring in his balls I squeezed them tightly and dropped the bombshell.'

'That was a brave thing to do.'

'I kid thee not.'

She took a long sip of her drink, licked her lips and said, 'I slid off the bed and put on my wrap and repeated myself again in case he hadn't heard me clearly the first time since he was almost seven sheets to the wind.'

'Then?'

'Well, he lay there in bed playing with his cock which was at half mast and wanted to know why I wanted to leave him.'

'And . . . '

'I told him I felt insecure and wanted something else.'

I visualized Menon lying in bed and going limp, scratching his balls and wondering what to say next.

Leela hadn't finished with the gory details because she went on and said, 'The lazy bastard didn't even bother to reply. He turned on his side and went off to sleep. By the time I reached the door to go to my bedroom, you know we had separate rooms, the fat slob was snoring.'

She snorted as if to say that was the end of the story and waved her empty glass in the air that Punditji refilled.

The above conversation was more or less a repeat of her earlier marriage break ups except in that her ex-husbands were, according to her, always heart broken, crawling on their knees asking her to come back and generally pathetic creatures. I had a momentary sense of pride in that Menon had not crawled and begged but had fallen asleep like a man. In my mind I said, Well done, you old sod.

'This was the ultimate insult. The son of a bitch went to sleep on me. I threw a slipper at him, missed as usual, and stomped off to my room,' she continued.

'Surely you didn't let it end at that, did you Leela?' I prompted her.

'Like hell! The next morning I went to see his lawyer and told him to draw up the divorce papers. I never hire my own lawyer. In these matters when you want to screw the old spouse always use his lawyer. That's my advice to all who want to go in for a divorce. You see, first thing is you don't have to pay the bastard a fee because it goes on the "party of the second half" account. The second reason is that the lawyer will try to get a big settlement so that he can get a bigger percentage. The buggers know that the wife has no money most of the time. So put the thumbscrews on the husband, is their policy,' she smirked.

I can see that a lot of people will consider Leela's attitude cold-hearted and mean. After all something that is supposed to have been made in heaven deserves, at the least, a warm funeral. But the truth is that marriages are not made in heaven but here on earth where considerations for a union can range from lust to love, greed to political expediency, shotgun affairs where the man is dragged to the marriage pandal or altar because he has had pre-marital sex and made the woman pregnant or for more practical considerations like dowries and rich fathers of ugly women.

That afternoon Leela was having lunch with a friend who was also visiting the town and around noon she said she was off. I warned her to take it easy on the hill roads and drive safely. All she said was, 'You bet. I love my life and I want Moron Menon's moolah.'

With Leela away for the better part of the day, she wasn't going to come back in a hurry, I looked forward to a much needed snooze after lunch. From what I knew of her friend she was also much divorced, a swinging socialite and given to bridge parties and the cocktail circuit. Birds of a feather congregate together, I mused, as Menon dressed rather nattily in a Polo shirt, cream chinos and white moccasins, freshly shaved and combed after a shower came and sat down.

'Where's Leela?' he asked.

'Gone to town to visit a friend,' I told him.

'I hope she gets tight and rolls the car off the road and into a khud,' Menon said fervently.

I looked at him quizzically and said, 'Didn't know you hated her that much.'

'Dammit. I want the bitch dead ASAP. If she doesn't croak I'll be out of a couple of millions.'

'Can't see that making much of a difference to your ill-gotten gains,' I said.

'Ill-gotten, did you say? I think I must tell you that every penny I earned was from sheer hard work. But I accept Balzac's saying that behind every fortune there is a crime. So, I see no reason not to admit that I have successfully evaded taxes, secreted some loot in Swiss banks and have built real estate. Anything wrong with that? Everyone does it, if you don't know,' he said and helped himself to a drink.

I considered what he had said and had to agree that what he

had done wasn't much of a crime when one looked around at the scams, rip-offs and kick-backs that made news from time to time. I knew most junior functionaries, there are almost four crore of them in the government, who had more money than I had and had assets beyond their official incomes. Yet, the larger, silent majority toiled hard to keep body and soul together. I was among them and so I understood what was going on around me.

Menon had possibly guessed what I was thinking because he said, 'The trouble with you dreamers is that you haven't any sense of psychology and how humans behave. If some beautiful woman walked up to you and flung herself into your arms you would, instead of making violent love, start jabbering poetry and making all kinds of promises of love-you-for-life type. People like you don't deserve any sympathy in my book.'

I suppose he was right because I didn't see any point in pressing my point about ethics and so on. He was a hedonistic man and like others of his ilk had no respect for opinions of others.

'You should get pragmatic,' he began again on his favourite hobbyhorse – psychology.

'You haven't, I bet, heard of Maslow's hierarchy of needs? I can see you haven't. This man wrote way back in 1943 a paper called "Theory of Human Motivation". It was his contention that once humans meet their basic needs they seek to satisfy successively higher needs that occupy a set hierarchy.'

I listened without taking anything he said seriously because he would often cook up all kinds of theories, quotes and so on to buttress whatever argument he was making. I am sure that there must have been somebody called Maslow but I hadn't read anything by him. I remembered Emmanuel Kant having said something similar. So I let matters ride.

'What hierarchy?' I asked to continue the conversation.

'Maslow's hierarchy is often depicted as a pyramid consisting of five levels. The four lower levels are shown as one group called "deficiency needs" while the top level is referred, as "being needs". Are you with me, so far?'

I nodded.

'Good,' he said like some professor addressing a class of

ignorant youngsters. 'The first of the basic needs is physiological, aiye eee, food, clothing and shelter. You know "roti, kapra aur makan". When some of these needs are not met, physiological needs take top priority. For example, what would you like on an empty stomach – love or food? Food is the correct answer. So love is pushed into the background. Recollect what that naked sage Gandhi said: I would reject God if he came to see me when I had an empty stomach, or something like that.'

'I agree with that,' I said grudgingly.

'Good. Now comes safety or security. This need ranks above all other desires.'

'Just a minute. Leela told me she told you she was leaving you because she felt "insecure". How come?'

'Yes, that's what she said. But she was making it up. That's why I didn't bat an eyelid when she came up with that reason. I said go and go in peace.'

'No, you didn't say that. You told her to fuck off to her latest lover.'

'Look, what's the point of discussing what has already happened. Now to get back to my friend Maslow, Abraham. He went on to explain what he called love and belonging needs. He said that once a person's security and physiological needs are met, a third layer of human needs becomes apparent. This involves the need for companionship (sexual and non-sexual and generally for emotion-based relationships). Humans want to belong to groups. Man is gregarious by nature. We also need to be needed. In the absence of this people tend to become susceptible to loneliness and social anxieties. Leela is a classical example.'

'Why Leela? Aren't we all? Look at you.'

'What about me?' said Menon.

'You are one lonely bastard. I bet you know that nobody loves you and you can't love anybody. In a sense you and Leela fall into the same category,' I said.

By then Menon was getting into his drinking stride that can only be described as fast and furious.

'You are one to talk. You have abandoned your natural companions, your family and in turn they have abandoned you. All you've got are drunk friends, like me, and some others. Okay, I'll grant you that you have a faithful hound and your Punditji. What else? No money to speak of. Your health is a dicey business and, yes, you have a creative mind. That's not too bad, what?'

'In vino veritas,' I told him.

'Don't throw your Latin shit at me. I know what it means. Speak plain English, will you?'

And, as an after thought, he asked, 'What does it really mean?'

I told him what I meant and he agreed. It was then that he came up with a monstrous suggestion that was to scar our lives forever.

'How friendly are you with the Doc who came in yesterday?' Menon asked.

'We are friends, in a manner of speaking,' I told him.

'Non. No. What I want to know is can he keep a confidence, a secret?'

'I suppose so. Aren't doctors bound by the confidentiality code?'

'They are supposed to. But in certain cases it doesn't quite work like that.'

'What do you mean?'

Menon looked over his shoulders in a conspiratorial manner made famous in Casablanca, the movie, stuck his face into mine and said in a stage whisper, 'Things like murder!'

'What murder . . . or rather whose?' I said in what I thought was a calm voice.

'That we will keep for later. Right now we have to make sure the doc knows how to keep his mouth shut.'

'Look Menon,' I told him, 'I don't know what cockeyed idea you've germinated in your drink-pickled brain. But I can't see me or the doctor being a party to it.'

'You will. You will,' he laughed loudly.

His laughter startled Doggie who got to his feet and moved a few steps away from us before flopping down on his belly again. The sun was overhead now and it was getting too hot to sit out in the open. Besides, I felt that we had had too much to drink early in the day and a meal was called for before the afternoon snooze. Besides, Menon's line of thinking was giving me the creeps. He was like that. Once he got hold of an idea he saw it to its final execution. But murder was another ball game and I wasn't inclined to be a party to such devious conspiracies. So I asked Punditji to give us some lunch. Menon declined to join me and I had some dal and rice and pushed off to enjoy my siesta.

Just before sleep overcame me I remembered Menon's words when he was summing up Maslow's theory. He had reached the part about esteem needs which he said were of two kinds. First, the need for respect and recognition by others. Secondly, self-respect. Then he had gone on to talk about 'being needs'. He said that while basic needs were deficiency needs and can be met and neutralized, they eventually stop becoming motivators in one's life. That is when 'being needs' come into play. He said self-actualization and transcendence are 'being' or 'growth needs'. He quoted Maslow when he said: 'A musician must make music, the artist must paint, a poet must write, if he is to be ultimately at peace with himself. What a man can be, he must be. This need is self-actualization.'

After what he had whispered to me earlier all this was sounding rather ominous. Perhaps, if he had suggested robbing a bank or kidnapping someone, I might have gone along with him for the sake of the thrill and experience. Or on his quest for self-actualization. Something like Don Quixote's Sancho Panza. But murder was something I had extreme aversion to. I felt no one had the right to take another person's life. But then Menon had all kinds of kinky ideas. At that time in his dissipated life he was into all kinds of kinky sex including pedophilia, homosexuality and other masochist fads. While he was in Bombay he was a member of a coven and there were rumours that he had started another one after moving to Delhi. This one had a tantrik thrown in for additional effect and members of this coven were seen hanging around cremation grounds looking for the odd unburnt skull to pick its brains for eating. Goddammit. Bloody cannibals.

Knowing Menon, anything was possible as far as he was concerned. Including murder. That's what made sleep difficult that afternoon. I tossed and turned around and drifted off into a fitful sleep that was far removed from the satisfying snoozes of the past.

I dreamt I was standing on the edge of a cliff and an eagle was asking me to come and fly with it. I wasn't too sure about it but jumped off the cliff anyway. I glided around effortlessly, swooping and pulling out of fast dives and then riding thermal after thermal till I reached the frozen heights of the Himalayas. I landed outside an ice cave and as I went into it I realized I was in the presence of someone else. In the gloom I could make out a naked figure of a bearded man with matted hair, eyes closed and icicles forming all over his forehead and face. I touched him and found his skin cold as the ice he was sitting on and it was then that I woke up with a start, sweating and shivering at the same time.

After slapping cold water on my face and combing my hair I proceeded to the glazed verandah from where I saw Menon fast asleep at the garden table with his head cradled in his arms. It was a posture one was told to adopt in any kindergarten school worth its name at the command 'finger on your lips and put your head down'. Obviously, he had been to one. His drink had spilled and the glass had rolled off and was lying at his feet. I let the sleeping dog alone and calling for Doggie went off for a walk in the oak forest that surrounded my cottage.

The air had become cooler and a smart breeze ruffled the oak trees. You could see the white dorsal side of the spiked oak leaves. It was getting on to sunset and Leela had not returned. I wanted to tell her about Menon's idea but I wasn't at all sure about who could be the intended victim. Was it Leela herself, his current mistress or someone else?

While I pondered this and strolled along, a pheasant ran across my path followed by her brood of chicks and a magnificent looking male. The hen was plain and ugly looking which is the case with the female of the species whether they are birds, bees, bisons or humans. I had observed that on numerous occasions but I had never been able to figure out what makes males run after females. Was it love or lust or the instinctive need to propagate or something more mystical? It was a passing thought because what really had taken over my mind and imagination was the murderous intent of Menon.

A walk in the hills as the sun is setting does several beneficial things. It gives the eyes, leg and heart muscles some exercise. Because of all the fresh oxygen being pumped into the brain, one's memory begins to work overtime and depending on the light and the mood it can be either nostalgic or happy or sad or precise enough for one to remember long forgotten arithmetic and multiplication tables. It also brings to the fore recent drunken conversations.

It suddenly struck me that Leela had said something about a great plan to screw Moron Menon before she left for her lunch meeting. But she had also said she didn't trust me and so hadn't divulged any details and the conversation had drifted off into how she broke the news of wanting to divorce Menon to the man himself. That's what clean mountain air does to you. Now I began wondering about what Leela could possibly be thinking of. She was one canny woman who possibly knew every devious trick in the book, and some not in the book. But murder was definitely ruled out because if she killed Menon then how would she get any of his moolah? After all they were divorced and she could not claim under the settlement any extra monetary benefits than the ones agreed to. One of these was an out of court settlement for which she had come up to my house to negotiate and which Menon said he was damned if he was going to give her a paise more than he already had.

Which meant Menon would have been in contempt and she could go back to court and demand all kinds of things. It would definitely be a long drawn litigation as courts tend to put such matters on the back burner and the lawyers have a field day making their fees at every adjournment. It was because of this consideration that the two had agreed on an out of court settlement which was not making much progress except for Menon's idea of bumping off someone, possibly Leela. And now confusing the scene further was Leela's undisclosed idea of shaking him down for a few million.

After I returned from my walk I found Menon munching a sandwich. Outside, Leela's Honda was parked and from all appearances things were just about returning to normal or what was passing for normal in my house. She was in her room, Menon informed me. His communication skills as far as she was concerned were either hand signals or pointed head movements with his eyes round and wide open darting in the direction of Leela like a Kathakali dancer. Sometimes he used his foot to point in her direction. This was very deliberate on his part and not just an act. It had subtle nuances and to the discerning few it was his way of expressing his deep disgust with her presence, her shadow and almost everything about her.

Leela was possibly sleeping off her lunch, which going by past accounts was one boozy affair. At any rate there wasn't anything new about it. Leaving Menon to his sandwich I went inside to my study and made a phone call to Doc Rawat. When I got through I asked him if he could meet me in the Sicoh Bar in town as I had something important to discuss with him. We decided to meet at 8 p.m. I changed from my crushed jeans into what I called town clothes, a blazer and grey flannels. Since I didn't own a car I had no option but to walk. It was pointless asking Menon for a drop to the town as he didn't like driving his Merc on the potholed road. Besides, one could never tell what kind of driving he was up to when he was sozzled.

In the bar, Doc Rawat had already ordered a drink by the time I got there. I ordered the same and without any preamble said, 'What would you do if someone told you he was going to murder someone?'

'That's an easy one,' he said. 'Tell the victim to scoot or get ready to fight back.'

'But supposing you didn't know the victim?'

'Well, there's not much I would do. Firstly, I would never go to the police because they don't take any cognizance of such raving and ranting. Secondly, I would keep my mouth shut and mind my own business. And that is my advice to you too.'

'That's no good. There must be some other way out. Can't the murderer or about-to-be murderer be persuaded to desist?'

'How? If the man or woman is serious about murder then not even god can do anything. Though in this case I don't think the man or the woman is serious enough. Potential murderers don't announce their intentions to the world. Neither do they threaten. They do what they have to, you understand. Only sometimes there are some people who botch up and make a bloody mess. But a clean shot to the head or a solid dose of some poison or the other does the trick. However, with poisons the problem is with having to get the victim to consume it. It is not always easy.'

Doc Rawat's wisdom was as good as my Doggie's. Even Doggie could have told me all that. The reason is that the municipality wanted to poison all strays and Doggie was one of them because he didn't have a collar and a license. The municipal dog murderers couldn't get a single dog though they got a few stupid cows and crows who ate their poisoned rotis. So, that obviously ruled out poisoning as a murder weapon. Now, shooting someone meant getting hold of a revolver which at the best of times was never an easy matter what with the stringent gun laws and so on. One could get an illegal weapon but they were not the most reliable and there had been reports of the guns blowing up in the hands of the shooter. That left knives and bludgeons of all kinds. I might have continued on this line of thought if I hadn't suddenly realized that I was thinking like a potential murderer. I told the Doc that.

'These things are known to happen when people carry heavy secrets,' he said and added, 'it's best you forget about the whole thing and now I've got to run.' He downed his drink in one gulp, as always, and was off. I stayed on in the bar and mulled over what he had said but unable to come to any conclusion ambled back to my cottage.

Dinnertime came and went and Leela didn't surface. Menon waited a while then said he was pooped and went to his room to sleep it off. I had nothing to do so I sat in the lawn and enjoyed the full moon as it sailed through a cloudless sky. The long shadows formed in the valley by the high east ridge melted away as the moon progressed high overhead. A flying squirrel launched itself from the tall oak that hovered over my cottage and glided off into the valley. The wind was blowing downhill as it always did at night and you could follow its path by the soughing sound it made as it rustled through the copse of deodars above my cottage. It was a soothing sound, gently rhythmic, almost like waves lapping a beach. I had often gone to sleep for short periods with this mystical music playing in my ears. The house was silent as a tomb, though the night was full of scurrying sounds in the underbush. A golden civet flashed across my lawn only pausing to glance at my reclining figure and darted into a clump of begonias. It was faithfully chased by Doggie who lost it when it climbed up the horse chestnut.

Seeing the futility of ever being able to catch the civet Doggie came back and flopped down at my feet. I could see his black pupils shining against the snow-white background of his eyeballs as the moonlight bounced off them. Good boy, I told Doggie to cheer him up at yet another failed attempt. There's always another day, I whispered. When the two of us are alone we often have long conversations with me doing all the talking and I swear the dog responds if you look closely at his eyes. We talk about this and that and I asked him the same question as I had asked Doc Rawat earlier in the evening. From Doggie's expression I gathered it was no point in getting involved with mad ideas and madder people. So what to do? I whispered. Let it ride, he seemed to say. His advice wasn't much different from the doctor's.

I can't recollect what the time was but it must have been close to midnight as the moon was directly overhead. A halo surrounded that dead piece of rock and I could see the man on the moon as he carried a bundle of firewood on his right shoulder. It was a picture-perfect moon, made prettier by a long flight of bats that silently sailed past it, their silhouettes stark black and the sound of their flapping wings drowned out by the soughing wind.

The door leading to the lawn gently squeaked open and I knew someone had opened it to come outdoors. I guessed it could be Menon or Leela and didn't bother to open my eyes. Doggie set up a low growling noise that forced me to open my eyes.

Framed against the high frontal profile of the house and descending the steps that led to the lawn was a ghostly figure enclosed in a cloak of blue flashing light. I blinked once or twice and then rubbed my eyes as the apparition came closer. I don't believe in ghosts because I know they don't exist. But at the same time I was quite prepared mentally to see one, some day or the other. Secretly, I wanted to see one as some people would like to see god before they believe in his existence. The strange sight or whatever glided towards me and as it came closer I sat up. Because the moon was directly overhead the face was shrouded in darkness but the figure was unmistakably human and when it said in a hoarse voice, 'Got a drink?' I knew it was Leela. That broke the almost surreal moment and I gave a short nervous laugh and said, 'You scared me.'

'Is that so?' she said in that irritating way most people use that particular question like they don't believe you or worse.

'You bet your beautiful arse,' I said, pissed off with her nonchalance that was mostly a put-on affair because people like her don't care either way for other people's feelings. 'As for the drink. You know where it's kept. Go and get it,' I said trying to get back at her but failing miserably.

'My, my! Someone is being petulant,' she said and gave her by-now-fully-patented crooked smile. In the light of the moon it looked a bit sinister. As usual I got up and went indoors to fetch her potion. I gave it to her and in a final gesture of defiance said I was off to sleep.

'Oh! Don't. I've got to talk to you. You are the only intelligent man around here,' she said.

I knew she was softening me up and so with a great show of reluctance sat down. I instinctively knew that something of interest would come out of that conversation. I needed to know what she had in mind rather desperately. This is an occupational hazard when one wants to be a writer and curiosity along with cats sometimes killed writers.

'Remember. I told you I had an idea to milk Moron Menon. I have worked it out and now I'm going to tell you because you promised not to tell him,' she said and sipped her drink, licked her lips, cleared her throat, lit a cigarette and said, 'How much do you want to know?'

'Well, all of it, I guess,' I told her.

In brief, Leela had worked out a plan by which she could blackmail Menon, and she had all the aces plus all the trumps. Many years ago someone had once told me about a certain part of the brain, I forget which one, which came up with these counter-productive ideas. Unlike suicide, that to my mind is in most cases a honourable thing to do, blackmail and kidnapping are dishonourable. One of my friends was a man, who I had never met in the flesh though we were bonded in our astral bodies, called Ernest Hemingway, who tired of writing blew his brains out. That was an honourable thing to do though a lot of his detractors said he was a coward. But try telling someone like Leela that and you will get an earful about middle-class morality.

She had told me that she knew where Menon kept his money in Switzerland. It was in a bank in Zurich on the Banhofstrasse and she had his secret bank account number because in a fit of drunken boasting he had shown it to her etched on the back of his gold Rolex. She had a photographic memory for numbers and had memorized it in one glance and then noted it down in a black diary, which she kept for addresses of people and such trivia. At that time she knew she would never get another look at the back of the watch as Menon slept with it on and did not even take it off in the bath. Her simple plan involved threatening Menon with government action unless he coughed up the two million she wanted. Whatever Leela's IQ, she was quite clued-up on what was going on around her. She knew that it was illegal to keep money abroad and under the Foreign Exchange Regulation Act, Menon could go behind bars for a long time. Menon was not going to relish the idea of being cooped up in a jail along with hardened criminals, eating jail food, denied his alcohol and cigarettes and women. He could, of course, give full vent to his homosexual fetish but then he would be opening himself to all kinds of diseases including AIDS. And the brutality that necessarily follows such action. Physical pain was an area Menon would go a long way to avoid.

'Imagine the poor bastard getting buggered by all those murderers and felons. It will be his nightmare come true,' Leela had said with some relish at that prospect. She could be very cruel hearted.

Since the whole matter was hypothetical I would have thought Menon would have agreed to Leela's demand after much haggling. There are some things all rich people fear in the country and they revolve around income-tax evasion and illegal funds stashed abroad. Naturally, Menon fell into the same category. But as I said, I would have thought, and that has nothing to do with what Menon thinks.

Leela had planted that nugget of information in my mind knowing fully well that I would blurt it out to Menon at the first opportunity. While I'm not a gossip I find that there are certain things I like to mention to my friends or whatever is left of them when I feel that their interests might be compromised. Leela was a shrewd woman and she knew all about that because of the many times I had told her of what Menon was doing behind her back and how and why it did not bode too well for their marriage. She had listened to me and instead of bringing up the subject with Menon she had increased the intensity of her promiscuity and instead of an affair or two conducted several at the same time. This she would then tell me in graphic detail on long distance phone calls that must have cost the cuckolded Menon a small fortune.

She knew fully well I would pass on the information to Menon. I would do that dutifully also aware that it made no difference to the old philanderer. Now that matters had come to a head and Leela was divorced and all, there was nothing further I could contribute in that direction to either of them. What they now did was their business and didn't affect the emotions and sentiments of either party or so I told myself. But blackmail was nothing I could condone or remain silent about. I could advise Menon to cough up and avoid the rigours of incarceration but then he wasn't the kind who listened to anyone. Yes, he heard them but it was a case of in one ear and out the other. Just the way his crooked accountants kept his books.

A false dawn was visible on the eastern horizon and the moon had ducked behind the western ridge. I decided to sleep on the matter and told Leela that I was turning in.

'Leave the bottle here,' was all she said.

The next morning Menon was the first to be up and about. I woke later than usual, around noon, and there was no sign of Leela. I noticed that Menon was sitting on my work desk and writing something on my typewriter. There was no telltale glass of vodka anywhere in sight. I was still in my pajamas and sipping a cup of tea as I walked across to pore over his shoulder at what he was writing. One never knew what he could come up with and perhaps he had hit on some bright idea for an ad campaign that would rake in more of the loot.

'What you looking at?' he said in shorthand.

'Oh! Creative master. Give us poor slobs a chance to see you at work,' I sniggered.

'Don't fuck around. This is serious stuff and meant for the likes of people like you who don't know anything but think they do. Now buzz off,' Menon said and dismissed me.

I buzzed off to my favourite place under the plum tree. The debris of the night before had been cleared by Punditji. The day's newspaper had arrived and was placed on the table. I glanced at the headlines. They were the same as any other day. Train crash somewhere, a bus rolling down the hill near Badrinath, father-in-law rapes daughter-in-law or father rapes daughter, the politicos having it out on the streets by engineering riots also called strangely enough communal. I would use the word to mean something done by the community for the community. As much as I like to believe that secular means non-religious. But newspapers had been using the words to mean something else. Communal was simply Hindu-versus-Muslim and secular stood for Leftists and Congressmen and non-secular for the Bharatiya Janata Party and the Sangh Parivar simply because they spoke of Hindu India and wanted to exclude everyone else from their concept of India. Then there were the backward castes, other backward castes, scheduled tribes and Harijans. It could get to be quite confusing to someone not initiated in the subtleties of the way life was in the country. Of course, people like Leela and Menon were out of the total gambit because these were meaningless things to them as they had nothing to gain on frittering time on such nonsense. What was more important for them was to figure out where the next million was coming from and of ways and means to blow it up in some degenerate way. It was what the Americans called the final cop out. I don't mean to run down my friends but I used to be a shallow creature like them before realization of some kind dawned on me and I began to apply my mind to the reality around.

Menon, however, was writing something about self-actualization and he stormed into the lawn waving a sheet of paper and asked me to read it. I took it from him and asked, 'What's this all about. Self-actualization?'

'Read it you dumbo,' he said.

So, I read it. It was an extension of the Maslow theory that Menon had been pounding me with over the last few days. His view or was it Maslow's, believed that self-actualization is the instinctual need of a human to make the most of their unique abilities. According to Menon's gospel, these kind of people embrace the facts and realities of the world, including themselves, rather than deny or avoid them. They are spontaneous in their ideas and actions. Further, they are creative. Menon said these people were problem solvers and frequently involved themselves in other people's problems. In other words, busybodies. This, Menon maintained, was the key focus in their lives.

The other parts related to how these people felt close to other people and generally appreciated life. Now came the important part and which was to become central to the events that unfolded in our lives. Menon liked to believe that these kind of people, obviously meaning himself, have a system of morality that is fully internalized and independent of external authority. Subsequent events showed that he was talking of being selfish, self-centred and devoid of any conscience or fear of god, the external authority. Finally, he maintained that they were not judgemental and therefore objective.

To me his morning creativity stank of some evil plot. He was a conniving man and a rascal to boot but people found him generous with his hospitality and liberal with his sexual mores. I was one of those who accepted him for what he was and refused to sit in judgement. Maybe I was objective, according to him or as he claimed, Maslow, Abraham. Every society has its demons and gods and while Ravana may be evil personified to those who think that Rama was an incarnation of Vishnu, he was according to many people a virtuous man who after kidnapping Rama's wife did not sexually exploit her while she was in his control. And here we have Menon in the same position as Ravana and by coincidence from the same part of the subcontinent.

The problem was that there was no Rama around to destroy this man with ten heads. I was no substitute and besides there was no Sita involved unless by some unimaginable stretch of the imagination the promiscuous and depraved Leela could be made to fit into the role of a virtuous woman. It was a scenario of its own kind. To resolve it one had to have Maslow, Abraham. on one's side. His was the voice that was driving Menon who fancied himself as a problem solver, unafraid of any external power, a man of independent morals or no morals and creative to boot.

'What were you and Leela talking about late into the night?' he asked suddenly.

'Weren't you comatose?' I asked him.

'Not as much as you would like to believe,' Menon said.

'Oh, this and that,' I said.

'You know you are a bad liar and that is the reason you will never make a good writer. Haven't you understood as yet that the greats of all times were magnificent distorters of the truth or reality. Take all those Russians, the French, the Irish and your best friend Hemingway. Liars all of them,' Menon said and spat.

'I thought you never made judgements. After all lying is only a sin in the West. Here no one gives a tinker's damn. Perhaps, you could be polite for once and call us writers creators of fiction that makes people laugh, cry and sometimes both. Or is that too much?' I said in defence of all those Tolstoys, Joyces and Hemingways.

'Stop waffling and tell me what Leela told you,' Menon said.

Like Leela he too had this uncanny gift of getting people to tell him their darkest secrets. I looked at his booze-bloated face, thinning hair and wondered where he had got the brains from. The son of a bitch must have selected his parents with great care. And as usual I told him what Leela had told me.

'The evil witch,' he exclaimed after listening to Leela's plot.

To myself I said, *Serves you bloody right Moron Menon.*

10

Shortly before lunch Leela announced she was going to the town to meet her friend. Menon said he couldn't care less and couldn't she just fuckin' stay away forever. I told her to have a good time. She smiled, winked and left.

'Wonder what she sees in that dumb cow?' Menon mumbled and signaled for a refill.

'Why? As far as I understand her friend is an intelligent woman, a practicing lawyer in the Supreme Court and into transcendental meditation,' I said.

'What rot! Anyone into TM and the Art of Living is a first-rate fool. These are matters considered in the religious domain, you should know. And anyone who is religious comes under the category of a sub-moron. I think you will agree,' Menon said with an air that assumes agreement.

'Religion is good for the people. It makes them feel secure and happy knowing that someday they will be rewarded in heaven for being good humans,' I said without any conviction.

'Yes. Yes! That's why millions all over the world are Christians or Muslims or Hindus and what have you. Nearly everyone wants to belong to one order or the other. Like those women who join the Rotary or Lions or Masons. Without a doubt most of them are suffering from some kind of insecurity coupled with guilt. I know quite a few of them. Hypocrites, the whole damn lot,' Menon roared.

This was nothing new coming from a man who had made his millions from duping people by creating needs that weren't there to sell rotten toothpaste, soaps, fizzy colas and such other consumer products. He wasn't alone doing that in an era of mass consumption but what pissed off people like me was the sang-froid with which he and his fellow professionals bulldozed their way through people's emotions and pockets. But then I was in a negligible minority and who cared for us anyway.

I mention this because Menon had said that I was a bad liar and hence couldn't be a great writer. He should know. He was in a business where lying had been made into a fine art complete with beautiful men and women, rosy-cheeked babies, clean and healthy looking thoroughbred dogs and such props that were used to sell anything and everything. Over the years the advertising world had become a sub-culture and its members another species or tribe that was marked by its customary arrogance and assumption that the consumer was a bleeding idiot waiting to be taken for a ride. They were like those micro-organisms called saprophytes that live off rotten and decaying plants. Barnum, who said a sucker was born every minute, should be having a good laugh in his grave at the way things are going in the twenty-first century.

Barnum apart, his reincarnation in the form and shape of Menon was having a good laugh, too. Now he was in splits about Leela's simple plan to blackmail him.

'Boy! Oh boy!' he said. 'The stupid bitch thinks she'll get away with it. Does she?'

'I suppose so,' I said, indifference writ large on my face.

'I suppose so!' he mimicked. 'When are you going to learn that I am a problem solver. I make a darn good living and plus out of it. Leela's intentions are all very well and possibly if it was some other arsehole she might succeed. But she has to deal with the likes of me.'

He then whipped out his mobile and dialed a number and said something in French. As I said Menon was a man of many parts and one of them was that he was a fluent linguist. He could speak French, German, Russian and American English like a native. I don't know who he spoke to and about what, but I guessed it had something to do with his bank account in Zurich. He gave crisp instructions and with an au voir switched off. No merci, so whoever he talked to was obviously some kind of a minion.

Then he asked for a drink and said, 'That'll fix the bitch! Go to the government, heh? Well, see about it.'

'What have you done?' I asked.

'I have suddenly made you richer by putting some money in your bank. You will get a remittance from Paris for five thousand US dollars for translation services for my company. Got it?'

'But I didn't do anything,' I said.

'Oh yes! You did. You gave me information. Forewarned is forearmed, you know,' and he laughed some more.

I wasn't going to kiss five thousand dollars away. I could do with the money specially as my publisher hadn't paid me my royalties for over a year and wasn't bothered about replying to my desperate messages about eminent starvation and death. Bad luck for Leela! She had enough money anyway and didn't have to be greedy. Mentally I converted the amount to rupees and was secretly delighted to find that I would be in bood and fooze for at least a couple of years.

'Thanks Menon,' I said.

I think he half expected me to refuse the money. But when I didn't make any of the usual noises about friendship and all that humbug, the bugger gave a smug look and his eyes said it all. I felt hollow and cheap. After all, Leela had confided in me and I should have kept her confidences. It didn't behove a man of principles to fall for the filthy lucre or so I told myself. To cover up my shame and disgust at the sordidness of the whole business I announced I was off for a walk and exited. Menon gave a limp wave as if to dismiss me as he had no further use of my services as an informer.

When Leela returned from her visit to the town she seemed to be in rather good spirits. We were alone for the time being as Menon had disappeared to do some work on his laptop. He always had the latest electronic gizmos and obviously enjoyed a mastery over them that made us computer illiterates rather envious.

'So you told him,' she said with that crooked smile of hers.

'Told whom what?' I said feigning ignorance.

'I knew you would. I'm talking about Moron Menon and what I told you last night about my plan to screw the bastard,' she said.

'Are you saying you knew all along that I would tell him?'

'Yes, you dumb twit. Can't you get it into your intelligent head that you were my via media. Now he is going to be forced into doing something. If he opens negotiations it will mean he will make a settlement. If he doesn't . . . well, I'll think of something else.'

Now I wasn't feeling bad at all about taking Menon's money. The crafty woman had been using me all the time and I had taken her at face value. Maybe I was a bigger fool than I thought. All the same, I vowed mentally to get even with her one way or the other. As things happened it worked out rather easily for me.

'Tell you what,' she said, 'go down to the valley or better still ring up some garage there and ask them to send up a mechanic to look at my car. I'm having some trouble with the ignition.'

I was used to getting instructions from her and so went and rang up the Honda dealer. He said he would send someone at the earliest that could, in our parts, mean an hour, a day or a week. I explained to him that it was urgent as the owner had to leave for Delhi. I then put on my town clothes and told Leela I was off to the post office to send some mail.

Actually, I was feeling humiliated, a fool and like a little schoolboy who is being used to fetch and carry. I was damned if I was going to let things slide so badly. I did have my self-respect if nothing else. I also had my own dog, house and a few clothes. Food I was assured for the rest of my life from the small rental income I enjoyed. So, why was I in such a rotten position, I asked myself as I trudged up the hill to the Sicoh Bar.

At times of great mental turmoil I escaped into the dark confines of the bar. I hung around with the low life where I could buy some respect by offering a round of drinks. These drinking cronies of mine were in the main junior clerks and petty contractors who were also small-time crooks and had long ago lost any sense of self-esteem. And they were more than happy to have me in their company because it gave them a sense of importance. They all knew that I was some kind of an important man somewhere if not in the town. The fact that I was a writer was known but then they weren't the types who read authors like me who wrote in English. Their reading habits were restricted to newspaper headlines and their talk revolved around who had done what with whom and such gossip which was by itself harmless but good enough to pass many a long winter day. No intellectual bullshit around here.

I walked into the cool of the bar and took my regular corner table. It was a quiet morning and on the table next to me a tourist couple was drinking beer and talking rather excitedly in what I thought sounded like Swedish. Raju, the waiter, brought me my glass of rum and as I took my first sip, in walked the usual bar flies, Roger and Harry. Roger was a clerk in the municipality and Harry was a photographer. Of course, their real names were Rajinder and Hari but I had anglicized them. They spoke English, in a manner of speaking. Like people who think in one language and then try and speak a foreign tongue.

My badly damaged self-esteem was in urgent need of repair and bolstered by the hope of seeing some real money soon ordered a drink for the two of them. Feeling more expansive I ordered a beer for the foreign couple.

There are some things that are good for your ego and one of them is flattery. So long as you don't take it too seriously and start believing the nonsense people say it works as a soothing balm to your sense of being. No sooner had the drinks arrived then Roger, consummate politician and courtier, complimented me on my blazer. It wasn't the first time and it wasn't going to be the last. He said I was looking 'andsome. I thanked him and reminded him that it was the 100th time he had said so. Harry not to be left behind asked me how much it had cost. I told him, as I had many times before, and Harry said loudly for all to hear that my blazer was imported from Italy. Then began a round of mindless gossip about the happenings in the town. Someone we knew had died the other day. He had hepatitis but continued to drink secretly, Harry told me.

'Daktor is sayings drinks bad for liver,' Harry informed me.

I told him that was true and he should take it easy as it looked like his liver was going to pack up any day. The two of them rattled away about totally inconsequential things and my mind went into a secret place where it didn't need to register what was being said around it. The rum was working slowly and methodically in dulling my pain of the morning and everything had put on a rosy hue. The Swedish couple asked if they could join us. Harry rose to give his seat to the blonde woman who thanked him and Harry gallantly said, 'ot at alls'.

They insisted on ordering a round of drinks for all of us and said they were Olaf and Sigrun from Greenland. I said it was quite far away from India and were they missing the cold.

'No, no,' exclaimed Sigrun. 'We like hot, what you say, weather?'

Harry asked them where their country was because he had never heard of it. 'I knows England, Zealand but Greenland? No knows,' he said.

Roger had a vague idea about the location and remembered something from his school textbook. 'Your house made of snow?' he asked.

'No, No,' said Olaf. 'Some Eskimos live in snow houz, igloo, called.'

'I sees,' said Harry who obviously saw nothing.

The concept of living in a house made of snow was mind boggling for him.

'Snow house, cold, no?' Harry said.

'Non, no,' said Sigrun.

'Not possible,' said Harry.

It was just the kind of conversation I needed to forget the ignominy of the treacherous house guests who were busy plotting and conniving at all kinds of skullduggery. Some times there are great pleasures in small things like the kind of talk the Greenlanders were having with Harry and Roger. English was a major casualty as they began to communicate with smiles, frowns, gestures and shrugs with some words of the language thrown in to give a vague semblance of a dialogue.

It was quite soothing to my ears and besides I didn't have to say anything. My mind drifted off into that safe recess at the back of my sub-consciousness, my face froze into a fixed smile and behind the dark glasses my eyes glazed over. It was the kind of drunk afternoon where one begins to drift without any thought for what may come next. Drinks were being knocked back with gusto and the Greenlanders had given up on the beer and switched to rum that they said they were drinking for the first time. The bar had begun to fill up with lunchtime tourists and it was becoming quite noisy. I called for my bill, paid and excused myself.

I ambled back to my cottage mentally quite restored to find a mechanic working on Leela's car. Since I don't know anything about machines I didn't even pretend to be interested. I walked on and into the house and to my room where I promptly went to sleep. I didn't need any lunch and told myself that Menon and Leela were quite capable of looking after themselves. Anyway, Punditji was around to see that they were fed.

11

This friend of Leela, who was also visiting the town, was introduced to a local tantrik who was an aghori or eater of dead humans. Most of Leela's crowd, including Menon, believed in the occult and black magic. Since Menon had refused to open negotiations with Leela on the out of court settlement issue, she had decided to put plan B in place. This plan, I was told, was supposed to cast a spell on Menon by which he would become subservient and pliable to all of Leela's wishes.

All Leela had to do was to go to this tantrik with a handful of rice and a rupee and quarter and he would do the needful. The catch was that the tantrik only performed at midnight. Leela roped me into the scheme and she told Menon that I had been invited to her friend's do. Ex-husbands were not allowed so he could jolly well stew by himself or get pickled or shag off. Menon, as usual, told her to go and stay gone.

We went in Leela's Honda to her friend's party where quite a few people, including some locals, had gathered. I was told in hushed whispers that the tantrik would arrive sharply at midnight and go into a trance. The party, as parties go, was nothing spectacular with the usual bar, food and some music from the sixties booming from a sound system. I did the obligatory jive with Leela and some woman she introduced me to and sat back in a corner to enjoy my drink.

This was a gathering of the rich and the odd celebrity visiting the town. In attendance were a painter, a wannabe writer, a television broadcaster, someone or the other who I was told was a film actor and some rather spindly looking females who supposedly modeled for a living. Sitting next to me was a retired chartered accountant who was telling all and sundry how he had come up with a scheme to plan everyone's taxes so that they didn't have to pay a rupee to the government. It was as interesting a scheme as any to evade income tax and for me it was a load of rubbish as I had no income and hence no taxes. The woman sitting next to me with whom I had had the last dance was a comely matron whose sagging breasts were held up by some kind of a miraculous bra but round her waist were the good old rolls of fat. Her sari was tied low down on her waist and her belly and navel projected themselves provocatively. Stretch marks on her belly were worn like surgical scars. I know men who liked such fat women. But from my experience they were lousy in bed because they laughed and giggled all the time while you strenuously tried to bring them to a climax. All that huffing and grunting would go to waste because the woman would never come and after you were spent, ask you rather odiously, if not sadistically, if you had enjoyed yourself. I had learnt long ago to stay away from them.

This fat lady, in particular, had diamonds sprouting from holes in her ears, nose and fingers. Every time she raised her glass to sip her drink her gold bangles would clash like cymbals and you had to but notice them. She asked me what I did and I told her flatly – nothing. Oh, she said, and turned her attention to someone sitting on the other side to whom she showed off her diamond rings. I could have bet my last rupee that the exchange going on between them was revolving around the price of diamonds, the cost of overseas holidays and such frivolous stuff with which the rich regale themselves.

From where I sat I had a view of the dance floor where some people were going through the motions of dancing but with little or no joy in it. The men were obviously husbands doing their duty and their partners wore the bored look wives reserve for their spouses in front of other people. For years I had been unable to understand why people did that. I mean exposing the hollowness of their marriages in public. They were palpably bored and given half a chance would have been off with someone or the other. The wives hung on to their husbands in quiet desperation because they feared the idea of divorce with all its implications of loss of face, chauffeured cars, unlimited expense accounts and all the paraphernalia that goes with being married to a rich man. The husbands reveled in the so-called sanctity of marriage because they could have all the flings they wanted without a sense of involvement or commitment.

The hostess had served an early dinner in anticipation of the tantrik's visit. To those not in the know, tantra is an ancient cult that originated in pre-historic India though some of the written texts available were probably written in the sixth century B.C. The word in Sanskrit means weaving and expansion. Tan means to stretch, expand, weave and spin out. The idea is to weave the disparate strands of our lives into one whole, grow and expand into joy. This pursuit of happiness is generally linked to sexual joy where physical senses become vehicles of liberation and enlightenment.

This, however, is a rather simplistic meaning that people like Menon would dismiss as ignorance. But then the world is also made up of Leelas to whom ignorance is bliss and it was into this bliss the assembled dinner guests were about to descend. The tantrik was a dark-skinned, horrible looking man wearing only a loincloth and with eyes as big as saucers. His face was fixed in what could be called a toothless, perpetual grin and as he stared at the guests through his bloodshot eyes most of them looked downward and one or two of them made to bow but the god man brushed them away contemptuously.

In his right hand he carried a drum and in his left a trident. He played it by rotating it and the strings with beads at their ends beat a loud and rapid tattoo on the goatskin stretched out on either end of the drum or 'dumroo'. This, the tantrik played from time to time as if to wake up all present. He was obviously a Shiva devotee with all the trappings of the god except for a coil of cobras round his neck. He only had one. The snake hissed and spat from time to time and to those afraid of that reptile cold shivers must have run down their backs.

The man sat down cross-legged on a deerskin placed in the centre of the floor by his disciple who then went and brought a square vessel that contained coal embers. The hostess had dimmed the lights and the guests sat in a circle on the floor. The tantrik had lit a clay pipe at which he puffed vigorously before exhaling a long plume of cannabis smoke. He then passed it on to his disciple who did the same and passed it on to the guest sitting next to him. The ritual required that the pipe be passed from person to person who in turn would take deep drags at it and exhale. Soon the room was shrouded in a sweet smelling cloud of cannabis smoke.

The tantrik played another roll on his drum and then intoned something in a monotonous voice before his eyes rolled upwards and he went into a shaking trance. His matted hair that was rolled up in a big bun atop his head opened up on its own and streamed down either side of his face and onto his shoulders. His head and body shook to the rhythm of the beating drum and the tempo was speeded up by his disciple who banged a brass plate with a stick. After a few minutes of this mesmerizing noise most of the guests had entered a trance-like state induced to a large extent, no doubt, by the cannabis.

Then suddenly there was silence and the tantrik said something. The hostess who seemed the most familiar with the ritual went to the kitchen and brought out a screeching chicken that the disciple silenced by breaking its neck. The tantrik ripped off the broken neck and drank deeply from the blood that spurted out of the neck and then passed it on to Leela who, surprisingly, also took a draught of it. Her eyes had glazed over and her motions were those of a deeply hypnotized person or someone who was sleepwalking. The tantrik then cast some powder into the burning embers before him and a loud flash resulted. That was the signal that the ritual was over and the tantrik rose and walked out as silently as he had come in.

Now that the first four of the rituals had been completed, that is, eating flesh, fish and meat (matsya and mansa), drinking wine (madya) followed by parched gram (mudra) it was time for the fifth – sexual union (maithuna). Leela had disappeared along with the tantrik into one of the bedrooms and the other couples were drifting off into the darker recesses of the house.

I could see that I had nothing to do there and pushed off to walk back home. Later, as was the routine, the hostess would switch on the lights once again. But the party mood would have mellowed somewhat and the sweet smell of burnt cannabis begun to cause mild headaches. The guests would gather their coats and umbrellas that they had brought because of a smart shower earlier in the evening and then in ones and twos they would ease out with languid good nights and see you's and much blowing of kisses at the hostess.

In the next couple of days there was no visible sign that Leela's spell was working on Menon. She would approach him with her offer and he would tell her to buzz off. After angry exchanges she would walk off in a huff and Menon would stick his tongue out at her retreating back. Sometimes he would give her the up yours sign by sticking his middle finger in the air and at times raise a clenched fist held up at the elbow by his left hand in the ultimate fuck you signal.

Eventually, I told Menon about Leela's plan to bewitch him. I described the tantrik ceremony and all that had transpired and he laughed. He laughed, loud and long.

'The stupid bitch,' he said. 'She got it all wrong. See, sometimes being parsimonious doesn't help. In case she had sacrificed a goat then we would have been at par because I have already done that to ward off spirits of all kinds. But the chicken she is, she went in for a hen.'

This was getting interesting. Here were reasonably educated and civilized human beings going in for rituals and beliefs that the most primitives of the primitives believed in. I laughed silently to myself to see this stupidity in action but I was also aware that the two of them were dead serious. Hoping to stop this ghoulish war I mentioned to Leela that her spell wasn't working because Menon had taken prophylactic action by killing a goat. She snorted at that and promptly went off to her friend. I understand she was advised to buy a buffalo and sacrifice the poor creature.

Near my house there is a temple where animals are sacrificed on a regular basis. Leela with some local help proceeded there with her buffalo and assistants in the dastardly act that was to follow. One of the eyewitnesses later told me that she personally severed the head of the buffalo from its neck with one slash of a khukri after she had gone into a trance aided and abetted by the tantrik. Then both of them bathed in the blood of the slain animal and copulated in front of all the others. The ceremony was as usual conducted in the dead of the night.

The way things were going these hysterical people would soon be progressing to pachyderms and whales, the latter, of course, not available in the hills or anywhere nearby but could be bought on the coast. Assuming they did all that and if even then the spells didn't work what would they do next?

Menon was showing no signs of relenting and Leela was showing signs of frustration and despair by breaking some more of my crockery and kicking out at Doggie more than once in a day. She had also taken to visiting the nearby camp of snake charmers and garbage collectors. Punditji informed me of this and said it wasn't good for my prestige to have my guests hobnobbing with the dregs of society. I couldn't have agreed more with him and said so to Leela who said she would leave if she wasn't welcome in my house. Menon was overjoyed when he heard her plans. I wasn't too sure. Leela had agreed to leave the house rather readily. There was something sinister in her hasty agreement to my suggestion.

After Leela had gone taking along her many suitcases there was a feeling of great peace all round me. I began to frequent my typewriter more often as I didn't have to sit out and keep both Leela and Menon company while they boozed away to glory. There was also a change in my drinking routine and I could safely say that I wasn't going around in some kind of a fog. Which was all very well because if it had been anything like what had been happening over the last few days the chances were that Menon would have been a handful of ashes flowing down the Ganga.

I think it was the night after Leela had left to move in with her friend in the town that Doggie nudged me awake to say that there was someone prowling around outside the cottage. Now Doggie doesn't bark like other dogs when he senses danger. He wakes me up with light taps with his forepaw and that is his signal that something is amiss. More often than not it is the neighbourhood leopard on the prowl.

I slid out of bed, picked up a heavy walking stick and slipped out of the house to circle around to Menon's side of the house. The room occupied by Menon had wide French windows that led to an open area that looked out towards the town. Since it was a hot summer Menon liked to sleep with the windows open so that his room was well ventilated by the cool night breeze. There I saw a figure silhouetted against the bright lights of the town poking what looked like a long stick or a bamboo pole through the open window and towards Menon's bed that was visible as a shadow in the night.

Before I could raise an alarm Punditji, who had crept up silently and was armed with an axe, struck at the foot of the interloper who with a loud scream of pain dropped the long pole and made a run for it down the hillside where he disappeared in a flash. We charged into Menon's room to find him fast asleep with not a care in the world. When I put on the lights I saw Punditji holding a long bamboo pole with which he rushed outside. I followed him to find out what he was doing.

Initially, I had thought that the man with the pole had come to rob Menon and before doing that silence him with a hard knock on the head with the pole. But it turned out to be quite different.

Punditji asked me to call the police because the man had been wounded and couldn't have gone far. I went to the phone and rang up the police station. About half an hour after that a sleepy looking sub-inspector with two other constables came to the house. I explained to him what had happened and showed him the pole that had been left behind as some kind of evidence. One of the constables looked at the hollow bamboo pole and warned his officer not to touch it. The inspector asked him what he meant and the man took the pole from him. He then removed what looked like a piece of dough from one end. As he did so a snake poked its head out and before it could come all the way out the policeman had caught it by the neck.

I stepped back in alarm and so did the inspector as he reached for his revolver. He was going to shoot the snake but the constable said it wasn't necessary as he had the situation under control. Then he told us a weird, though interesting story.

He said he came from a village near Bijnor where there was a colony of snake charmers. Besides, gathering alms and money at village fairs and from homes these snake charmers caught snakes found in people's homes and fields, sold venom and, more importantly, for a suitable price used their expertise to kill people. The killing-the-people part had our attention instantly and all signs of sleep disappeared. The modus operandi, he said, was to put a live snake inside a hollow bamboo and seal both ends with dough. Then at the right moment insert the bamboo through a window or a hole in the wall into the victim's bedroom, preferably the bed itself. But before doing that the dough is removed from one end so that the snake can slither out directly into the bed of the person to be killed. After that the snake does the rest, he said, and showed us the cobra's fangs. Then after it has done its job it leaves the scene and no one is the wiser.

The inspector looked at the constable as if he didn't believe him. I, too, found it strange that anyone would want to kill Menon. Anyway, the inspector said he would like to catch the perpetrator and the three men set off to track down the assassin. As they were leaving I mentioned helpfully that there was a colony of snake charmers living near my house. Having said that I nearly bit off my tongue because it suddenly struck me that Punditji had seen Leela hanging around with this particularly unsavoury lot. Now just because she had been mixing with snake charmers didn't make her guilty of having paid off a man to kill Menon. Or did it?

I thought about that part of the fact and came to the conclusion that had the snake bitten Menon he would have been another statistic of those bitten by snakes all over the country. There would be no suspicion on anyone, least of all Leela who was not living in the house anymore. And after Menon's death Leela would possibly inherit all his millions because he had disinherited his children 'because they were idle bastards living off him', as he put it.

I also remembered that Menon had mentioned that he needed to change his will but had been too busy to do that because of the divorce proceedings, work and other such things. In effect, Menon's sudden death would benefit those mentioned in the 'will and last testament', as he grandly described it. Leela was bound to be one of them, one could safely bet. And there was every chance the woman knew all about this. But murder? Well, here was another Lady Macbeth floating around except that in this case it was all for her personal benefit. And this one was smarter than Shakespeare's villain because she chose such a devious way to kill instead of the good old dagger.

It was getting on to first light and Punditji had brewed some tea when surprisingly Menon walked out of his room and joined me in the verandah.

'What was all the commotion about last night?' he asked.

I told him.

'No kidding?' he said.

'No kidding,' I assured him.

He thought about that for a while and then went indoors. In an hour or so he came back shaved and bathed and dressed in a smart bush shirt and cotton khakis. He asked Punditji to put his suitcase in the boot of his car and without much ado announced that he was 'off'.

'Where to?' I asked him.

'Somewhere. Far away from that conniving bitch,' he said.

Menon running away? Was he scared? Most unlike him, I told myself. I sensed the crafty old bugger had something much more sinister up his short sleeves.

'Well, have a good trip and drop a line once you get somewhere,' I said.

'See you, when I see you,' he said and walked away to his car. I went to see him off and before he let in the clutch he said, 'If you see a Mallu and snake crossing the road in front of you, kill the Mallu first.' Now that could have meant anything and it was typically Menon to make fun of his own community. However, it sounded ominous all right given the events of the night. I could see the bugger was building up a homicidal rage.

I saw the rear of his car vanish around the bend in the road and thanked my lucky stars that nothing untoward had happened under my roof.

In the house the phone was ringing and I went in to pick it up. It was the police inspector who wanted to know if he could come over and ask me some questions. I told him to do that. I knew he would have by then visited the snake charmers' camp and gathered some information on the memsahib who was seen recently there. Women like Leela don't, as a rule, visit slum dwellers. She was no social worker and slumming wasn't one of her hobbies.

The inspector came and joined me for a cup of tea. I asked him if he had any news of the wounded interloper of the night.

'Oh him! We caught him even before he got back to his camp,' he said.

'Oh!' I said fearing the worst. 'What's his explanation?'

'The usual.'

'What's that?' I asked the rather complacent inspector.

The police officer told me that the man was a petty thief and had hoped to pick up some valuable odds and ends on his nightly rounds. He had chanced into my house and seeing the open window wanted to steal Menon's wristwatch and wallet that he had seen was lying on the table next to his bed.

'Is that why he was sticking the long pole into the room?' I asked.

'More or less. That's how they rob things like clothes and articles lying around.'

'But the pole had a snake inside it,' I reminded him.

'The snake? Oh, that was just his pet,' he told us.

I found all this rather mystifying. The assumption till then was that the man was an assassin hired to bump off Menon and it was more likely a Leela-initiated-and-bankrolled plan. We talked some more and he suddenly asked me if I had any other guests.

I told him I had but the lady had left the day before and was probably staying with a friend in the town. He asked for the friend's address and I gave it to him. I asked him why he wanted to meet her and he said it was routine. Then he rose and went away.

The more I thought about it the less I liked his explanation. The police can be a devious lot, a characteristic that comes with the job. Wouldn't you if you spend a large part of your time chasing criminals of all kinds? So, there I was stumped as usual and finding myself rather out of place. I don't like that at all because it is like walking naked on the Mall in the middle of the day. In passing the officer had said that they had let the man go as there was no point in arresting him since nothing had been robbed. The wound on his leg had been treated at the civil hospital in town and while he may have to limp around for a while, it was nothing serious.

Leela had left the day before and as always without a good-bye or a thank you. I learnt this when I rang her friend up. I wanted to tell her what Menon had said about Mallus and snakes and to see if she could throw more light on the subject.

It was a few weeks after Menon and Leela had left my little bungalow on the top of the hill and I was enjoying the first showers of the rains that had begun earlier than usual. In the hills the monsoon comes in waves of massive clouds that burst with unrestrained fury, threatening to wash away everything in their path. The dry storm drains gush down like mini torrents and each year they erode another part of the land. Landslides block traffic on main roads, sometimes for days. Huge swaths of mist swirl in and out of the vales and across the dales and a carpet of green grass covers the mountains almost overnight.

Underfoot, leeches are born from eggs left over from the last rains and moths bounce of the streetlights. In a lull in the rains cicadas set up a mad chatter and birds come out in dozens to dry their feathers. Fireflies can be seen at night zipping around in the darkness. But the best part is the sonorous rattle of raindrops on tin roofs that can easily put you into a sleepy mood if not make you downright lethargic.

Children wade through drains on their way to school and back home much to the consternation of their mothers who can't figure out how water gets into their gumboots. Wet clothes take days to dry because once the rain sets in it can go on for days without a break. A sunny day is an instant holiday and people's clotheslines are full of laundry hung out to dry. In that brief period of bright light people squint and blink as they come outdoors after having being cooped in the darkness of the blankets of mist. The lichen on the rocks shine like emerald velvet and somewhere the brain decides that it is a moment of cheer and one feels invigorated and all set to go for long walks. Thunder lilies break out in pink rashes and wild dahlias punctuate the green-carpeted hills like motifs on expensive silk. Primulas – pink, red, pinkish white and sometimes with a dash of yellow – bloom in the shadows of boulders.

It was that kind of a sunny day when I got the call from New Delhi. I was cheerful and happy after almost two weeks devoted to my writing without any disturbance or interruption. I planned to meet some people I knew in the town but the phone call called for a rapid change of plan. It was Menon.

'Can you get your bloody arse down here instantly?' he said.

'I could but what's the rush?' I asked.

'I'll tell you all that when we meet. In the meantime pack up. My car is on its way to pick you up. And don't worry about money and things. I'll take care of all that.'

With that he put the phone down and left me as confused as I could be. He had, I mean Menon, that rather irritating habit of assuming that everyone was at his beck and call. For a moment I considered an open revolt, but only for a moment. After some thought I went to my room and put together a few shirts and trousers, socks and the manuscript of the book I was working on. Of course, the trusty portable had to go also. In a manner of speaking I was on his payroll and couldn't forget that he had gifted me five thousand dollars at a time when I needed it badly.

Shortly after breakfast Menon's Mercedes rolled in. His uniformed chauffeur saluted me smartly and asked if I was ready to leave. Punditji picked up my bag and stowed it in the back seat.

I like to ride in front or as the Americans say shotgun. I enjoy the ride better and can feast my eyes on the lush green fields of sugarcane and rice as the car flashes by splashing muddy water on people walking or cycling along the road. I know they don't enjoy that at all because when one looks back one can see them gesticulating and hurling abuses. But the car is too fast for them and the sound of their angry voices fades away till the next such incident. In the ponds and flooded fields buffaloes wallow chewing cud with a stupid and peaceful expression on their face. In some places young, naked boys sit atop the animals and use them as diving boards. Sometimes the sun comes out from behind a bank of clouds and its reflection bounces of the paddy fields in bright bursts of light. In small towns along the highway or what the narrow, potholed road is supposed to be, markets draw the villagers for their weekly shopping.

In the Mercedes the ride is smooth and as comfortable as it can be. After a few hours the city of Delhi appears in the distance. Multi-storied buildings reaching for the sky like erect penises of some supine giant. Or giants. There are so many of them. Then come the ruins of the Old Fort, Sher Shah Suri's citadel and a host of tombs of well known and not so well-known kings, Sufi saints and many of the characters that made Delhi what it is. A city of ghosts and others trying to get into that ethereal world double quick. In our lifetime we had already seen two assassinations, one of the father of the nation and the other of 'India is Indira and Indira is India'. Then there were the thousands who died during the Partition and after that in what are called communal riots. And before that there had been men like Nadir Shah who put hundreds to the sword in one night of bloody frenzy. Then there had been the English who blew people up from the mouths of their canons simply because they had had the temerity to rebel against them. Outside police headquarters, a flashing signboard tells you how many people have died in road accidents, so far. It is one bloody place, New Delhi is.

Meanwhile, another supine giant, without an erect penis, was lying on his stomach on the floor of his drawing room in a palatial house in Defence Colony. It was Menon in a lungi, bare-chested with his belly hung in loose folds that jiggled every time he spoke or moved. When I said 'Hullo' he simply waved me to a chair nearby, rolled over on to his back and precariously balanced a glass of amber liquid on his belly button. His Man Friday, Swami, similarly attired and with a bigger pot belly and arms where the flesh hung loosely and with caste marks prominently displayed on his forehead was pummeling and massaging Menon's rolls of fat. He finished whatever he was doing with a loud thwack and came and gave me a toothy grin. Then he served me a glass of the same amber liquid that Menon was drinking.

I took a sip and said, 'Hm. Good stuff. Glenfiddich?'

'So, at least you know your malt,' Menon said.

'I have a passing acquaintance from the old days when I could afford it,' I told him.

'Your problem, my friend is that you have chosen to be a writer instead of the brilliant copywriter you used to be. Now it was your decision to wear that crown of thorns. So if you bleed don't expect any pity from me.'

'Balls to you, Menon,' I said and drank the malt in one go. Swami refilled it.

'Yeah! Yeah. Balls to me? Remember what I told you about us Mallus. Forewarned is forearmed. Just remember that, you silly bugger.'

'I've heard that crap over the years so it doesn't impress me. Anyway why have you summoned me?'

He scratched his balls, an old habit which was supposed to signal that the man was in deep thought. Actually, it was a great diversionary trick because everybody sitting around him would look at his hands and miss the look in his eyes. It was what many pipe smokers did, fiddling and farting around with the gadget or lighting and re-lighting their pipes.

'Oh, yes!' he said after a suitable pause. 'The reason you have been brought here kicking and screaming is to be told that Leela is no more.'

'What? What do you mean she's no more? You mean like she's out of your life or what?'

'Oh, very much so. She's completely out, erased, deleted, wiped off, scrubbed out. Whatever you like,' he said.

'Well, that must be quite a relief,' I said.

'Yes, and no. You see, she's buried six feet below where I'm lying and from where I am getting a reverse isometric view of your thin legs,' the man said.

I suppose I, as they say, looked aghast. My mind went into overdrive and then it short-circuited and went into a blank mode. I reflexively reached for the malt and drained it off.

Swami refilled it and said, 'Leela Mem no more. Gone to patal.'

He grinned mirthlessly and pointed to the floor where Menon lay on what was an expensive and brand new Kashmiri silk carpet.

Patal is where the God of death Yama lives somewhere in the bowels of the earth and I must have got over the initial shock to comprehend that these two fat men had murdered that woman. From what they were saying they had then buried her in the drawing room where the Kashmiri carpet was draped over the very spot like a chaddar at some holy man's grave. Except that there was no monument to mark the grave but for the flat floor and the carpet.

I rose, somewhat shakily, prompting Menon to sarcastically remark, 'The malt too much for you?'

After pacing the room for a while I regained some composure and enough to tell Menon that he was a murdering swine. To which he laughed and said a swine is a swine, murderer or not.

'Now you are an accessory after the fact, you dummy,' he said.

It was his way of telling me that if I ever spilled the beans on him I would, like him and Swami, also be behind bars. That was a sobering thought. I excused myself and went to the bathroom to wash my face and get some kind of control on my trembling limbs and rattled mind.

On my return I saw him on his favourite sofa, his fat, bare feet beating a soft tattoo on Leela's grave.

'I won't tell you why I killed her,' he said quite calmly. 'However, I'll tell you all the gory details of how I cracked her head with Swami's staff. And believe me that people who say they don't remember what they did in anger are liars. Bullshitters, I tell you.'

He took another swig of his whisky, cleared his throat and resumed. 'The staff cleaved her head into two along the lines of the central parting of her hair. Her eyes popped and her mouth opened to scream but no sound came. She sank to her knees and along my arms I felt the vibrations travel to my palms. It felt as if I had just cracked a soft-boiled egg. Her brain spilled over and rivulets of blood ran through the grey mass. Swami took the staff back from me and administered the coup de grace. See, now you know exactly how it happened. Don't ever, I repeat, don't ever make me tell it to you again.'

My stomach heaved and I felt a burning sensation in my esophagus as bile moved from my stomach into my throat in one big reflux. I ran to the bathroom and threw up violently. Then I washed my face in cold water once more.

There was no chance of getting any light thrown on Menon's remarks about Mallus because Leela was buried deep in the darkness of the grave. Besides, Menon had rather crudely told me what he had done. Now she was interred in his drawing room with all her and his secrets taken care of. When Menon shuffled off to take a shower I lifted one corner of the Kashmiri carpet in the fond hope that he had played a dirty joke on me. No, sir! There was a slab of fresh marble placed in a regular oblong to match the other marble slabs in his drawing room. If one didn't know better it looked no different from the older slabs. Just a bit more highly polished and less used. The carpet covered up that deficiency quite neatly without upsetting the ambience of the room. The bugger's homicidal rage had exploded.

My nerves had been restored enough to let me focus on the matters at hand. Surely, I reasoned, Leela gone missing would have elicited some response from her friends, house staff and others who she met on a regular basis at her kitty party and bridge club. But then it might not have. She was known to disappear for long periods without telling anyone where she was going. It was only when she returned that her friends would know about her exploits in Paris or London or exotic places like Kenya and Bali.

Menon, of course, knew that very well and must have taken it into consideration before bumping her off. That sounds crude but I imagined Leela bludgeoned to death with hard hits to her head leaving goose bumps all over me.

That Swami was once a professional wrestler and despite the flab was actually quite a strong man who on more than one occasion had doubled as a bodyguard for Menon. Among his various jobs in the house one was to throw out pestering and unwanted females that Menon had got tired of. He did that by simply packing their bags and shoving them out with sound slaps to their bums.

I visualized him finishing her off for sure by crushing Leela's head with one hit to her head with his iron tipped stave that he kept in a handy place behind the door leading to the drawing room. Since it would have been impossible for Menon to have dug the marbled floor it must have been left to Swami to do the hard and sweaty job.

Again, I wondered what the neighbours had made of all that digging and hammering noise. But in Delhi neighbours believe in minding their own business to such an extent that if a woman was being raped in front of their eyes they would do nothing about it. Forget murders and murderers. It is easily one of the most selfish and anti-community minded group of people anywhere in the world. There are several reasons for it but primarily it is because Delhi is made up of migrants from all over the country who come here to make a fortune. Very much like Dick Whittington and his cat. In that quest of happiness, here happiness and money are synonymous, no one feels it necessary to be diverted by mundane stuff such as murders, wife beating husbands, cheating wives and so on and so forth. Gone are the days when the poet Amir Khusrao said Delhi was a city of dreams. It is now more a city of nightmares.

Menon came out of the bath in a silk dressing gown and went to the air-conditioner where he opened the front and let the cool air waft over his belly, balls and breast. Swami had placed another glass of malt in his hands and as he looked at it raised to the light said:

From what dripping cell, through what fairy glen,
Where 'mid old rocks and ruins the fox makes his den,

Over what lonesome mountain,
Are you come to me – Sorrowful me?

'You're waxing poetry,' I remarked.

'No. Reciting it. It is some drinking song from Ireland or Scotland,' he said and added, 'there's more to it, if you care to listen?'

'I couldn't care less. So you buried Leela?' I said.

'Had to. She died, you know,' he said rather peevishly.

'Died? You mean murdered by you and that oaf Swami,' I reacted sharply.

'Hey! Hey. Keep your temper and sense of holier-than-thou to yourself. Your glass is empty,' he said and snapped his fingers at Swami.

I had a feeling that the malt was an insidious brew. Someone had made it in distant Scotland where murder was as common as Haggis, where Lady Macbeths prowled the corridors of dark and dusty castles clutching bloody daggers and shouting 'out damn spot' and where ghosts appeared around every corner and at every banquet. Somewhere in the back of my subconscious and malt-free mind I wondered what happened to hope, faith and charity, and I told Menon so.

'What rubbish? That is all very well for Christians. They can keep their faith and charity. And also their Kingdom of God, postal address unknown and no internet connectivity.'

'But, dammit . . .,' I stuttered.

'A man must have many vices,' he pronounced, 'or be damned for all his life.'

It was one of those pointless arguments with Menon. He knew and I knew that I would cave in like a house of playing cards before the onslaught of his logic and verbosity.

'The easiest thing in the world is to choose a vice. There are so many of them. Fornicating, seducing other men's wives, buggering a child and getting buggered in turn, playing the horses, fudging accounts, worshipping the devil and then there is this,' he said holding up his glass to the light and striking it sharply with his thumbnail to make a melodious tingle. 'The good old fail-me-never.'

'You must be sorry for yourself,' I told him.

He only laughed.

'We know each other too well. Look around and find out the sort of life I live before jumping to conclusions.'

Menon was a hard-hearted man and a villain to boot. I had had enough of him for that morning. I asked him if I could be dropped off at the Press Club where I still had a membership that I could afford.

'What for? You don't get Glenfiddich in that watering hole,' he said.

'I am only doing what you said I should. I'm going to look around.'

He waved his hand at Swami who led me to his car and as I closed the door behind me I heard him yell to the driver to stay with the sahab till the cows come home.

At the Press Club I ran into the regulars from the *Hindu* and sure enough Raja, another mountain man and a senior crime reporter, propping up the bar. He was genuinely delighted to see me and so were his chums who had enjoyed the largesse of my unlimited expense account in the good old days. Now I was a struggling writer holed out in the hills and scared of venturing outside. But I had my ill-gotten gains from Menon burning my pockets and as in the old days ordered a round for everyone I knew which was almost the entire standing population of the bar.

The lunch hour crowd was a much more subdued lot made up mostly of senior journalists, PR men and the advertising wallahs. Politics and cricket were the sole topics worth discussing and sometimes there would be some office gossip but in the main it was all predictable stuff. I liked that because it kept my mind off the horrendous goings on in Menon's Defence Colony mansion.

I didn't feel like I had been away for almost five years and that is what I like about places like the Press Club. Sure there had been some changes. The club now had better furniture and the staff wore clean uniforms. And on the walls were photographs of members who had passed away, some of them quite recently. It was a safe bet that they had died of cirrhosis of the liver though one could hear words like liver cancer, hepatitis, heart attack and such other complications of the human body being used as euphemisms for alcoholism. There would be a rare case of someone copping it in a road accident but the whisper would be that he had had one too many.

Before Menon had made his big bucks he was also a regular here. Now it was below his station in life to be drinking at cheap dives like the Press Club. He frequented the Captain's Cabin and such other fancy and expensive bars where he entertained owners of the media and not their hired help. But all the same he was a well-known figure.

When I told Raja I was staying with him all he said was that I was a lucky bugger. 'Plenty of booze and women,' he observed.

I gave them that half laugh which means neither yes nor no. Of course, the assembled company assumed I was having a ball.

Since I was in a splurging mood I invited some of my drinking companions for lunch at Karim's in the Jama Masjid area. We packed into Raja's clapped-out Fiat and drove through pools of water and a light drizzle to the Old City. There in the shadow of the gigantic Jama Masjid we parked and walked the rest of the way and through a narrow lane to Karim's. It was my favourite eating out place in Delhi. The food was delicious and if you didn't mind the flies, open drains and general stink that pervaded the place you had a jolly good time. In my times it was a fashionable place for those wanting to slum around or pretend to be more ethnic than the locals.

It was a sumptuous meal and I tucked in knowing fully well that it might be a long time before I got another opportunity. That overeating and boozing in the monsoon humidity and heat took its toll and by the time I reached Menon's I was gripping my stomach that was churning and threatening to explode. I rushed into a bathroom, let down my pants and passed out happily on the w.c.

It was dark when I woke up. It took me time to figure out where I was but eventually I recalled and groped around for the light switch. With the light on I saw I had messed my trousers and there was a terrible stink all round. I stripped off and ducked under the shower and soaped myself vigorously. I came out of the shower feeling very much like a new man and generously slapped some after-shave lotion that was kept in the bathroom cupboard. I needed to get to my room to change into fresh clothes. I left the dirty and soiled ones on the bathroom floor from where Swami or someone would collect them and send them to the wash. Wrapped in a towel I stepped out to hear voices in the drawing room. I tiptoed my way to my room that was on the first floor and changed into T-shirt and jeans. I had a pair of sandals kept for the hot weather and wearing these came down to the drawing room.

Menon was sitting on the big leather sofa and on his lap sat his current mistress. She was holding his glass of whisky from which he took occasional sips.

Seeing me he said, 'I heard you shat in your pants.'

'You heard right. I think I've got an attack of the good old Delhi-belly.'

'Well, nothing like a straight shot of good old Scotch to fix it. Help yourself,' he said and pointed to the bar in the corner of the room.

I didn't think it was such a good idea but considering the medicinal properties and a cure for my misbehaving stomach I went for it. The woman had smiled at me in recognition though I would have thought that Menon had most probably reminded her. She was one of those gaga women who giggled all the time without a sense of mirth. She also had a high-pitched and rather nasal and irritating voice. Her favourite expression was 'super'. Menon called her dumpling and I think her name was Sonu or some such.

Viewing the two of them from the distance of the bar I thought this was most bizarre thing I had seen. Menon's fat feet were resting on the Kashmiri silk carpet covering the tomb of the late Leela. Dumpling or Sonu was mooching around and Menon had one hand inside her blouse. I wondered if there were things like ghosts and was it possible that Leela was drifting around watching the scene and thinking of some way of spooking them. I wouldn't have been surprised to learn that Menon had been screwing his mistress on top of the tomb of his murdered wife just to get more even with her. And sure enough I wasn't because he slid down from the sofa and stretched out on the carpet with Dumpling riding him and going at it with great enthusiasm. I watched for a while from my corner and since I don't enjoy being a voyeur, took my drink and went and sat on the lawn outside.

Swami came and sat down on the ground and began to massage my feet. He was good at that and by way of small talk he advised me to avoid eating out in Delhi and stick to his cooking. He was a rather good cook and some of his Malayali dishes were out of this world. Specially, his fish preparations.

'So, Swami you sent Leela mem to patal,' I said.

'God's will, saar,' he said.

'You know that is murder and you can go to jail and, worse, be hanged if you get caught.'

He grinned and said, 'God's will, ji.'

After living in the north for some time now he had picked up the servile mannerisms of menials and would always complete his sentence with a 'ji' that was a mark of respect but when he said 'sir ji' he was being obsequious. That was what one had to look out for. It was true that Swami was Menon's flunkey. But he was also his own man and had an ego as big as his master though he made sure that it never came through publicly or in front of people he considered superior in rank. He had come into Menon's life as a young fugitive from a village close to Menon's home in Kerala. He had run away from home after killing a cousin of whom he was jealous because he was successfully courting another cousin who Swami loved rather desperately. The girl, a pretty girl ready for marriage, always treated Swami as a buffoonish brother who was only good at eating and wrestling.

Whereas, the man who had her affections was a scholarly type destined for great things in life and had plans to finish his university education and become a teacher. Here Swami was at a disadvantage, as he had no plans to be anything but a wrestler. Frustrated at the girl's intransigence he killed his cousin in a fit of rage. Then he made a run for it all the way to Bombay where he landed at Menon's doorsteps and asked for sanctuary. Little did he know that he had sold his soul and made a pact with the devil incarnate.

In many ways I sympathized with him because I was finding myself getting increasingly compromised. The problem was I didn't know how to get out of the mess I was in now. If I had not come to Delhi at Menon's command and rebelled, I wouldn't have known about Leela's horrible murder at his hands or at his behest. Then I would have been a free agent and could go about my business without a care in the world. But it was money and money alone or rather the lack of it that had landed me in this mess. In a way both Menon and I were victims of circumstances brought about by that magic word called money. He, because he had too much of it, and me because I had none. Neither of us had a leg to stand on in the eyes of the law though we could soothe whatever was left of our consciences by justifying homicide as a necessary tool to carry on with our pursuit of happiness.

Perhaps, Swami read my thoughts. He made to get me another drink but I refused. What's the point? I asked myself. I mean worrying about what had happened. If that was my destiny, so be it. Why buck it? This convoluted logic soothed my frayed nerves and since I can only fight stress by taking long walks I set off to have a dekko of the neighbourhood.

15

When I came back from my stroll I found that Menon and his mistress had left for a night out. Swami said I could join them at the club if I wanted. I told him I didn't want and instead called up my ex-wife who said she would be quite happy to see me and maybe we could have a meal or something. That something part always puts me on high alert. Some ex-wives want to pretend that nothing has happened and life is hunky dory. That is the civilized way to go, I am told. Despite the years of separation I always felt a little sad that things would have been better had I done this or that. All the ifs and buts rankled my mind but since I had learnt the hard way that it was futile to think about what had happened and there was no way the clock could be turned back I let myself drift with the tide.

She had some friend over who I was told was some bigshot in some company or the other. Under different circumstances I would have been more civil but I wasn't in the mood for polite conversation and so sat silently sipping my drink.

'Sue tells me you are a writer,' this Mr Kapoor told me.

I shrugged and gave him my short laugh.

He persisted and said, 'I always wanted to be one but you know how it is in the corporate world. No time for such creative pursuits.'

I don't know what its about people but whenever they meet a writer most of them turn around and say they also wanted to be one. But they couldn't for one reason or the other.

Unhappiness is writ large on their faces as if they have missed the biggest vocation in the world. Some of them go to the extent of saying that they would chuck up all their wealth and material belongings at a drop of the hat and bugger off to the mountains or the coast to write. In only one instance do we have a story by Somerset Maugham where the protagonist flees a middle-class world to set himself up in Paris as a writer, or was it a painter? So did the Black writer Jones, the whitest of them all Hemingway and before that the Fitzgeralds, Virginia Woolfes and such other products of the American middle class. I've heard of some Indians who also followed suit but in the main they were painters though there could be a writer or two.

I told the gent from the corporate world that anyone can write (paraphased the famous quote: there's at least a novel in all of us). That he should try his hand at writing by moving to an unheated London attic and making the rounds of the literary agents and publishers there. Just to prepare him for the rigours ahead I warned him that life was hard and English landlords and landladies were tough nuts who hoofed out defaulters without much ado. It would, of course, help to have an English mistress. And just to steer him in the right direction I told Mr Kapoor that English women had a thing about us Indians and if nothing else he was assured of regular sex and various varieties of it. The idea was to take the Mickey out of him and Sue caught on fast. After all she had seen me doing this a dozen times with many a pompous ass.

She tried to change the subject and said, 'Talking about overseas. You know what the children are calling me these days.'

'What,' I asked.

'Ghouly,' she said triumphantly.

'Ghouly? What's that supposed to mean?' I asked.

'It's from ghoul, ghost, silly,' she said.

'But you are alive and kicking. Is it some kind of a nerdish expression?'

My children, who were infact thirty-odd-years old and adults with minds of their own, were doing quite well for themselves abroad and with time their visits home to their mother and me were few and far between. We kept in touch though. They by telephone and SMS and I, old-fashioned and silly, wrote long e-mails which they rarely bothered to answer.

'No. It's a form of endearment, you see. I think they think I haunt them.'

That was quite true. My former wife was one of those mothers who hang on to their offsprings all gooey and gushy, refuse to acknowledge that they are in their thirties and keep reminding them not to pick their noses or some such stuff. Bloody irritating when you are some kind of a responsible adult with lots of people taking orders from you. And, in turn, you have one or several bosses haunting you day in and day out. And here comes mother with her homilies about time to settle down which is double speak for 'get married before it is too late', eat on time and don't eat junk food and so on. No wonder the kids called their mother a ghoul.

Talking about ghosts, I told Sue that Menon's ex-wife Leela was dead and we could call her 'ghouly' in the real sense. Sue had never liked Menon. First, because he had never made a pass at her and secondly, she envied his capacity for making megabucks. She would always bring this up when we used to have a spat. 'If Menon can do it why can't you?' was her refrain. To which my standard answer was that I was not Menon and he was not me.

'I hope she haunts that black bastard,' she said with vehemence.

Kapoor raised his eyebrows at this use of unladylike language. But obviously he knew Sue only superficially. I wondered if he had managed to get into her panties as yet. Possibly not because then he wouldn't have been surprised. Sue used some rather endearing expletives when making love which would make the ears of many a bazaar whore turn red and make many a sailor blush.

After some other small talk Sue said that she and Kapoor were going out for dinner. Kapoor gallantly asked me to join and I said I didn't want to be a bone in their kabab and besides my stomach wasn't up to a meal in a restaurant. I asked Sue to call me a taxi. This, I must point out, is perhaps the only civilized thing about Delhi. I'm told that taximeters are fixed on the higher side and taxi drivers are big cheats. However, you can get a taxi day or night on the phone and that is perhaps the only thing one can say in defence of Delhi's cheating cabbies. With see yous and the obligatory kiss on her cheek I left.

In the taxi, as we moved towards Menon's mansion, I wondered what Sue did with her time besides being courted by rich corporate types. She was still well preserved and attractive and made for good company at a dinner table or on a date. She had never worked and had no experience of any kind that could get her a job. I was given to undcrstand that shc was somc kind of a lobbyist, dabbled in real estate and one of her visiting cards said she was a realtor with a foreign degree in the subject. The foreign degree part puzzled me because as far as I knew she had never been abroad. I assumed that it was one of those degrees Americans keep throwing around by post. Or mail order, as they call it. For money she didn't have to worry too much as her doting father had left her a fortune. I was ruled out as a source of support because I was broke, unemployed and did not have a chance in the world of ever having any real money.

I got off at Menon's and before retiring for the night asked Swami to give me a glass of lassi to make up for the loss of fluid caused by a misbehaving stomach.

16

The noises of a city waking up, the roar of buses hurtling down empty roads, cars being warmed up for the day and such alien sounds woke me up earlier than usual. I lay in bed and wondered what the day had in store for me. One thing was for sure that Menon would not surface till noon and then immediately rush off to some meeting or the other.

I walked over to the drawing room and the dining area next to the kitchen where Swami was already brewing coffee. The rich aroma filled the house and I asked Swami to give me a cup. I sipped the coffee and looked out at the back garden where bougainvilleas were in bloom and small birds were darting in and out. I think Swami kept a plate full of bird food or kitchen leftovers that attracted these birds. Suddenly a flight of pigeons landed and the little tits and wagtails scattered in all directions. There was much pandemonium in the little garden and the cause of it was the appearance of a stray cat that made the pigeons head for the sky. It all made for delightful viewing and also for a bit of thought about nature's ways. But before I could really sink into the luxury of being philosophical, Menon made a surprise entry.

He plunked his coffee on the dining table next to me, drew up a chair and gave me a gruff good morning. I looked at him and gave a faint smile at his tousled appearance and blood-shot eyes.

'Rough night, eh?' I said.

'Umph,' he said.

Swami had placed the morning papers next to me and Menon grabbed them and hid his face behind them as he went through each one of them at a page turning and burning pace. From long practice he knew what to look for and that were the ads placed by his company. I don't think he ever read the news, specially none of the stuff about politics and the pontificating editorials. In his hand he had a red pencil with which he made quick slashes and underlines that were no doubt meant for his underlings to pay attention to. And the newspaper reading session was over even before he had finished the first coffee of the day. From long association with him I knew he would regain some sense of the normal after his second coffee and so let my eyes slide over the headlines.

Right on schedule that is, after finishing his second coffee, Menon asked how I had spent my evening.

'I visited Ghouly,' I told him.

'Who the hell is Ghouly?'

Menon prided himself on knowing everyone by name and face and that by itself was quite a talent. I told him that it was the nickname for my ex given to her by our children.

'But she has a perfectly good name, Sue. Why Ghouly?'

'Apparently she haunts them or rather tries to be overprotective and issues them instructions that they don't want to hear or something like that.'

'Haunts them? I suppose she's like most fretting mothers and there's nothing wrong with that,' Menon said.

All said and done, if he had really loved anyone it was his mother. I remember the binge he went on after she died. It was nearly a year before he sobered enough to take control of his affairs. And any talk of a dead Amma, his or anyone's, brought tears to his eyes. Even Indira Gandhi who he possibly hated very much.

'No. Nothing I suppose. But they are no longer children, for god's sake. They are in their thirties, old enough to do as they please, don't you think?' I remarked.

He dismissed my argument with a grunt and reached for more coffee.

'Have some more,' he said, 'good for your Delhi belly.'

That morning it was not my Delhi belly that was a source

of worry. It was the hollow feeling in my stomach. A hollow feeling brought about by the knowledge that I was an accessory after the fact to murder. And here I was sitting with the murderer and drinking his coffee. In plain English – I was in a blue funk. The last time I had had that sensation was when I bunked school and knew what the consequences would be if I was caught. Both at the hands of the Headmaster and my father. Mercifully, I had got away but that sensation had remained and I stayed away from any kind of wrong doing for a better part of my life till that instance.

I wanted to get out of Delhi as fast as possible and I said so to Menon.

'What's the rush?' he said nonchalantly.

'Well, I haven't got anything to do here and the heat and humidity is doing me no good,' I said.

'What do you mean you've got nothing to do here? I have called you down because I need your support to tide me through what could be very troublesome times if the police even get a whiff of what happened to Leela.'

'How would that happen?'

'Oh! In many ways. We are not out of the woods as yet. Suppose her children or her former husbands start making inquiries. They are still besotted with her, you know. And they'd love to get even with me, the bastards.'

That was a distinct possibility, and at some time or the other a dead certainty.

'What about Swami?' I asked softly.

'Him? Nothing to worry about. He's smart enough to keep his trap shut, like you.'

I wasn't too sure about myself. I couldn't picture myself running from the police, forever looking over my shoulder, breaking out in cold sweat every time I saw a uniform. I simply wasn't cut out for that kind of stuff. I knew I would breakdown the moment someone asked me a question. It wasn't that I thought of myself as a weak-kneed individual. But I was no good at telling lies and as Menon had said it was because of this that I would never be a great writer. Writers must be skillful liars, he had said repeatedly. But a coverup was needed if I was to stay out of the gallows.

'Why don't we leave the country for a while?' I suggested.

'That, my friend, would be an admission of guilt. One can't suddenly up and bugger off in the middle of a murder investigation which is bound to take place sooner than later.'

Some friend, I thought to myself. But I had to hand it to him, he was a cunning son of a bitch. What all this meant was that I would have to sit it out, sweating and having nightmares. Good-bye writing and all that. I had been handed over the job of holding his hand, of course, for a price.

He asked me if I needed the car to go around during the day. I told him I was staying put and would catch up with some reading and watching television. He went upstairs to his room and I gazed out at the lawn and watched the cat among the pigeons and wondered what would happen to me if the cops caught up with Menon. Would I keep flying from spot to spot, always on the run never knowing where my next drink or food was coming from, if at all?

My thoughts wandered here and there and I fancied myself as a man on the lam being chased by hordes of cops, always outwitting them and like the Scarlet Pimpernel, one step ahead of the hangman's noose. My imagination was let loose on this scenario and I pictured myself drinking absinthe on Paris pavements one day, knocking back beers in London pubs and martinis in New York bars. Basking on sunny beaches in Tahiti or some island paradise. The last one appealed the most. Of course, all this was being done on Menon's money.

My line of thinking was broken with Menon announcing he was off to Mumbai and would be back in the night. People like him were commuting to all points of the compass like they were taking local buses to work. That says a lot for the aviation business. And for their money, of course.

I looked at him blankly and he spun on his feet and was out of the house with Swami lugging his big black briefcase. I knew he used to hold meetings at airports all over the country with the local branch managers waiting in attendance to bring him up to speed on various projects. Sometimes I wondered why he hadn't bought a Lear jet or something like that for himself since that was what successful tycoons acquired after making their first million or whatever.

And then I was back to morbid thoughts of what would happen to me after being nabbed. I looked at the colourful silk carpet and the dreadful secret that it covered. Did Leela die painfully? Was it a clean hit to break her skull like an eggshell? Or did Swami make a mess of it? I imagined the blood spattering the floor and the walls. I had read about how forensic experts could detect signs of blood years after a killing using ultraviolet lights like restorers do with old paintings. Did the Indian police have such expertise? To reassure myself I assumed that they didn't, and so detection of the crime from that angle was ruled out. I made many such reassuring discoveries as the morning progressed and with each one I felt better and was soon hollering for my breakfast.

At around noon the phone rang and I heard Swami answering it. I had just then poured a beer for myself and was enjoying its delicate aroma and flavour, it was imported after all, when Swami said if he could trouble me to answer the person on the other end of the line. The request was immediately followed by that nervous apprehension that whoever was on the other end could be trouble. I took the phone from him and said 'Hello' in the faintest voice I could muster.

'Speak up, please,' said the embodied woman's voice.

As a rule I like to hear most women on the phone because they sound so sexy and beautiful even if I know they could be fat, cross-eyed, balding and so on. This was a hangover from the days when they had telephone operators with whom I would flirt on the phone trying to kill time in some seedy hotel room in some miserable mofussil town where I would be visiting either to do a survey or find out what had gone wrong with our advertising campaign. It was a harmless pasttime at least till the operator played the game. I knew so many operators by name that it wasn't funny. I kept a small diary where I would log in such encounters and rate them. The best ratings would go to the girl who talked the longest and I would make it a point to ask for her at the switchboard. Sometimes the names were pseudonyms just like today's kids at call centres who use nome de guerre and phony American accents. And I would have to strike them from my diary. But most times I hit the jackpot.

To get back to the voice on the other end. It was melodious enough though pitched too high for my ears. So, I said hello once again but with greater authority and volume.

'Is Leela there?' said the voice.

'Who?' I parried.

'Leela Menon. And who are you anyway?' said the woman.

'Oh, that Leela. She isn't here and hasn't been here for months,' I said.

'And who may you be? And where is Menon?' she persisted.

'A visiting friend,' I said skillfully, evading a straight answer that came from long practice with such calls and before the woman got too inquisitive I told her that Menon was out of town and would be back sometime later in the evening.

'I said who are you?' the woman went on.

It would have been easy to get out of the conversation by giving her my name and ending the call by saying the appropriate good-byes. But telephones are just too sophisticated these days and I knew the easy way out would only mean the woman would re-dial and re-dial till she got an answer from me. She appeared to be that kind of a woman, very much like a terrier who doesn't let go the bottom of your trousers once he's sunk his teeth into them.

'May I know who's calling?' I said in my most civilized voice.

'I am a friend of Leela called Misty by friends though my name is Mishti, you know sweet,' Misty a.k.a Mishti informed me. One thing was established. The lady was a Bengali or a Bihari because it is only in the eastern part of the country that girls get names after sweets, flowers and such delicate embodiments of the female. That is why I am from the school that believes that girls are really sweet only up to they are three year old. Once they get conditioned by their mothers, they turn out to be exact replicas that can range from raving lunatics to frigid, impossible to be satisfied in-and-out-of-bed females. This cloning is done invisibly and subtly and that's why I tell any young man who wants to get married – look at the mother of the girl carefully because that's what you are buying, my friend.

'I am a family friend,' I repeated in a voice that made it clear that I do not wish to give Misty my name, profession and address.

But Misty obviously wasn't the type who gives up easily because she then wanted to know how come I don't know her. I explain that away by saying that our paths might have never crossed. Of course, I'm wishing fervently that they never do and for god's sake will this pesky female get off the phone. And then I come up with the great idea by announcing that there's a call on line two and could she call Menon in the evening.

I switched the phone off and retired to my corner of the drawing room from where I couldn't see the silk carpet, took a long swallow of my beer and returned to my copy of Jug Suraiya's latest book. He's the kind of writer who lifts the spirit when one is feeling down and haunted by all kinds of dark thoughts.

I put the call out of my mind for the time being but soon I put the book down and began to concentrate on a niggling idea. Suppose that Misty wasn't satisfied by my evasive stuff and decided to pop in. What would be my line of action? I could disappear upstairs and claim I was unfit to meet visitors. But would that not only confirm the impression that I was trying to evade, hide? And wouldn't Misty wonder why I was doing something like that? I bet she would. She seemed to be that kind of a woman. And another bet, an exact replica of her mother who ever she was. She would quiz Swami about the mysterious family friend and I wondered if she was one of those women that Swami had sent packing. Then I would be out of my misery because I doubt if she would dare to enter the house. But suppose she wasn't? All this supposing was getting me down and with the intense heat being generated in the old nexus that I feared I would soon have a calcination of the brain.

This fear of calcination of the brain brought back distant memories of writings by another anarchist. Way back in the sixties and seventies it was the thing to posture as an anarchist and not an atheist. Atheism was a thing of the past and one of the notable thinkers was a Polish dissident with an unpronounceable name, but called himself Wlodek to make it easy for chaps like me. He propounded the concept that the idea of a Lord God was a political one. Self-indoctrination, according to him, is most dangerous. You can make others believe many things and you can believe anything, he argued.

What I liked the best about his line of thinking was his praxis that avoiding the company of 'bad' people was egoism because it only gave 'salvation' to his or her arse. Mind you no talk of soul here. He was also great on forgiveness, a precept I followed in my own matter with my ex-wife. The argument was that two people were needed to commit a sin. Let's say murder. Then the murderer is one person and his victim the other. According to him, the very act of not forgiving those who trespass against us is 'participation'. I think he meant that we became murderers or the murdered by not forgiving either party.

A bit convoluted and confusing line of thought, but all the same in my those troubled moments it came as a soothing balm to my fear of calcination. To those who don't know, calcination is an alchemist's way of converting base metals into noble ones. But calcination of the brain is another ball game because it can cause seizures and eventually attacks of epilepsy. And with those rather unpleasant thoughts circulating in my mind I decided to seek a change of scene and asked Swami to call for a taxi to take me to my favourite watering hole – the Press Club.

Menon blew in late in the evening, breathing hard like he had walked to Delhi from Bombay. He was all for making dramatic entries because he said people only paid you attention if you put on a bit of histrionics. I raised my glass of malt to acknowledge his appearance. My gesture was studiously ignored because he was talking on his cell phone. If one didn't know better one would have thought the man was barmy because it appeared as if he was talking to himself. Another miracle of technology. A latest version of 'Mama look! No hands'. Swami had placed a drink in his hands and in between his animated conversation and much waving of his free hand Menon would take a sip as he prowled round the drawing room.

When he had finished talking he said, 'How was your day?' and answered it himself by adding, 'Quiet, eh?'

'Somebody called Misty rang up asking for Leela,' I told him.

He stopped midway from taking a sip of his drink, 'Shit! Not that bitch?'

I shrugged my shoulders and let him expound and expand on that. I knew he had much to say about this Misty female because he had stopped pacing the room and plonked himself on his favourite sofa with his feet resting flat on the silk carpet that covered Leela's grave.

'That cow is another mistake from my unholy past,' Menon said. 'I ditched her for Leela and instead of taking it badly she teamed up with her rival and both of them ganged up against me. Such then are the furies of women scorned.'

'So?'

'So what? They became thick as thieves. Always together and I am sure plotting and planning against me all the time.'

'Menon, you are being paranoid,' I said.

'What? Me paranoid? I am telling you the two must have tried to kill me at least on two occasions.'

'How?' I wanted to know.

'How? Hey, Swami tell this sahab here how they tried to kill me. Didn't they poison my drink with something called sulpha, a bloody pesticide, for god's sake! Took me for a pest, they did. It was Swami's acute sense of smell that saved my hide. He knocked the drink out of my hand before I could swallow it. Now, didn't you Swami?' he said.

Swami dutifully shook his head which is quite misleading to those not used to southern mannerisms. Down south they signal agreement by moving their head sideways. That, you should know, is the universal signal for a nay.

Menon and Swami were one of a kind. It was difficult to make out which one of them was a liar. I think they were partners in crime and Swami who played his role of a faithful and loyal retainer to the hilt was invariably part of anything Menon said had happened to him. Menon, to make his point would often ask Swami to corroborate. This was a trait one can see among some married couples where one agrees to substantiate what the other is saying knowing fully well that it is a bag full of lies.

'And the second time?' I asked.

'Swami, tell him. No, hold it. I'll tell you. This was on a holiday in Kashmir. We had rented this shikara houseboat called "Abdul's Paradise" on the Dal Lake. Leela had insisted on taking Misty and her son, some guy in theatre and fashion, who was a raving queer. We made quite a foursome and that houseboat rocked to our lovemaking. I think I buggered that queer more times than I laid either Leela or Misty. Anyway, to keep it brief, one night when I was well gone on charas and booze the three of them tried to push me into the lake. Leela knew I couldn't swim and if it hadn't been for Abdul the

Bulbul, the owner of the houseboat, I would have been found the next day floating with my belly up.'

'Wow! No kidding?' I said.

'I kid thee not,' Menon replied.

I then knew I was in real bad company but remembering the Polish pop philosopher I decided to stay on and not indulge in egoism. And anyway what could have I done? I could have made a run for it back to my cottage in the hills. That would have been dangerous because Menon would and could set Swami after me and I too would bc buried in my own bedroom. I could go to the police but what was the point. No one would believe me. I could inform the ex-husbands of Leela but that would only complicate matters and implicate me. I stopped thinking because I feared calcination of my brain could happen at any moment and I would lie on the carpet convulsing, writhing and moaning like an epileptic.

For people like me to stop thinking is like going to sleep. It rarely ever happens and even in my sleep the mind is busy dwelling on one aspect of one thing or the other. I am not a worrier and I still have a healthy crop of hair on my head to show off while my peers have balding pates. Menon is a case in point. On the surface the man appears to have not a single worry but deep inside he's a very worried and worrisome man. His excessive boozing, womanizing and other peccadilloes, his understated boasting about his business acumen and so and so forth are all manifestations of his worried brain.

And, now he had a murder and that too of his former wife to worry about. By burying her in his drawing room he had not entirely eradicated her from his memory. It was a stopgap measure and he was the kind who'd wait for something else to come along before getting rid of the feeling of having done anything wrong. He was definitely not familiar with the word guilt as it is generally understood. Remorse and regret were for the birds in his lexicon. Live for the day from day to day was his motto.

The next morning, after glancing through the entertainment page of the *Times of India*, I took a leaf from his book and decided to go and a see a Naseeruddin Shah production of *Gandhi*. The performance was in some local theatre and I wondered if I would be able to get a ticket. I mentioned it to Menon who rang up someone and a ticket was delivered by lunchtime. Menon had as usual disappeared to Bangalore or some other place and was not expected back till the next day.

The play was thought provoking because it was about one facet of Gandhi's personality that was generally not talked about in public. It was his lack of understanding and compassion for his eldest son whom he treated rather harshly, or so it was portrayed in the play. Did the father of the nation have no time or love for his son? He may have had at sometime but he appeared no different from most domineering fathers and husbands. His personal life was rather selfish though we have been told that he sacrificed it for the nation. His ascetic lifestyle, his fasts and his unabashed fondness for Nehru were in most people's minds the hallmarks of a saint. But the play made him out to be an ogre and one came out of the theatre with the impression that if there was one person who did not consider him a saint then it was the author of the play.

It was more fun worrying about the Mahatma's chinks than Menon's. Did the Mahatma die with a guilty conscience? I didn't think so. There couldn't have been time for remorse or regret after the bullets entered his wasted body. His was the kind of death most old people would like to have. Instantaneous. But old age has its spin side and that possibly explains why some old farts are such grouses, ill-tempered and demanding individuals. I could see Menon fitting into that category very well. But the son of gun had no one, except Swami and me, to be near him in his dotage. Why me?

I had in more ways than one sold my soul to him. I knew that there was no question of redemption of my atma and it would like many a haunted spirit flit from place to place, drift through cold wastelands and burn its way through unending deserts. It was a prospect that frightened me. And because I was frightened I did what I had learnt a long time ago from my boxing coach, a retired Anglo-Indian sergeant. Offence, he had said, is the best form of defence. I thought up a scheme by which I could defraud him and disappear forever from his world into a world where he couldn't reach me. But then as the saying goes the best-laid plans of men and mice . . . or is it mice and men?

What I wanted to do needed a collaborator. I had to find a partner in crime and wracked my brain for old names that could come in handy. I had the whole house to myself as Menon was away in Bangalore or Chennai. Whoever I recruited had to hate Menon very much and while on this line of thought it struck me that Misty could make a suitable associate. After all she had hated him enough to try and kill him not only once but twice and in cahoots with Leela. That she saw him as someone despicable wasn't in doubt. So I mulled over the fact that here was a scorned woman, an unsuccessful murderess and someone itching for revenge.

I had no such intention and my motivation was more activated by the fact that I wanted to get away from Menon's clutches. The man had fast become like the Old Man of the Sea in Sinbad's adventures. He wouldn't get off my back and the only way to get rid of him was to drown him in the ocean. I was thinking metaphorically.

I knew that what would hurt Menon the most was a raid on his bags of money. Anything else wouldn't make him even bat an eyelid. He had no sense of self-respect, pride or noblesse oblige. Misty after much thought was becoming a viable candidate for my devious scheme.

The more I mulled over the choice the more I became convinced that salvation lay in making a deal with Misty. The problem now was: how to contact Misty? Using Swami's help was out of the question. Making a cold call to her may not prove very fruitful as she may choose to give me a cold shoulder. After all I had not been very forthcoming or helpful to her when she called asking for Leela. It came to me, like it used to come to Prophets of old, a vision of things as they should be.

In this vision I meet up with Misty on the excuse that I have come down from the hills and have been given her number by Leela who was till recently a houseguest. As I am a bit lost in the big city could she take some time off to show me the sights or something on those lines. It sounded quite good to me. But I needed her number. Menon had a phone where one could scroll for numbers of received calls. I did that and found several numbers which were local calls. I started calling all of them one by one and soon hit the jackpot on the third or fourth try.

It was Misty herself. I began my spiel and she said she had heard of me from Leela and I said the usual banal stuff about 'good things, I hope!' And she said of course. Apparently, Leela was all praise and described me as some kind of a literary giant, genius and such adulatory words. My self-esteem shot up a few notches. So did my courage. I could now safely ask for a date and did so without too much ado. We decided to meet at Gaylord's in Connaught Place for cona coffee that afternoon.

I had arrived a bit early and taken a table from where I had a clear view of the door. Just a few minutes after our scheduled meet a woman walked into the restaurant. I didn't have to make two guesses as to her identity. She was big in the bosom and wide in the shoulders; round faced with dimples and a hairstyle that I understand is in fashion though it looks like a kind of a beehive. Her sari was tied low on the waist and rolls of fat lined her waist and a wispy blouse struggled to hold her mammaries in place. She did a survey of the room with her chin held somewhat imperiously like in statues of Queen Victoria and with a 'we are pleased' expression strode to my table. I was easy to recognize in my long hair, beard, T-shirt and jeans. I stood up and we shook hands while a waiter held a chair for her into which she flopped with a loud whoosh.

'It is hot as hell outside and no parking. I had to walk all the way from what's-that-place-called where they have set up a parking lot,' she began.

I gave her a sympathetic look and agreed it was too hot to walk even if the distance was only about fifty metres. Her eyes had adjusted to the dim interior and she gave me a thorough look over. She must have liked what she saw because she said that Leela hadn't mentioned that I was also a good-looking man. My self-esteem again went up a few notches. The waiter brought the cona coffee and a plate of assorted cakes. Misty didn't waste much time and helped herself to a black forest and a lemon tart and tucked into them with a schoolgirl's delight. No wonder she had rolls of fat where her waistline should have been.

In between mouthfuls she asked what had brought me to Delhi. I told her some bullshit about meeting a publisher. She didn't care for that bit of information and merrily stoked her belly with some more black forest. All this time I hadn't even had a single pastry and she had gone through three of them. Expensive woman to keep, I thought. When she had finished her second cup of coffee richly laced with cream and several cubes of sugar she pushed her plate away and leaned back to give a lazy, satiated smile.

'That was super,' she said.

'Have some more,' I said encouragingly.

'Oh, no!' she said and patted her swollen, fat belly.

I poured some more coffee and asked her if she could take me around to the usual tourist spots like the Red Fort and the Kutub Minar. I saw her hesitate and to lead her on said I had a car at my disposal with a driver and she wouldn't have to worry about driving and parking and so on and so forth.

'That would be super,' she said and grinned from ear to ear and large dimples formed on her fat cheeks. A smiling Misty was quite a tolerable woman to look at if one ignored her beady eyes sunk in layers of fat, totally devoid of any emotion. Cold as a snake's eyes, I observed to myself. This was one party one had to be very careful with, my instinct told me.

It was late evening when we left the restaurant to the parking lot where she had left her car. Mine was parked at the same place and she said she would like to drop her car home which was on the way to the Kutub Minar. I got in with her and she roared off into the heavy traffic, switching lanes and honking incessantly and cursing other drivers. My car was following but I bet my driver couldn't have driven the way she did. Boy! oh boy! I told myself as I grimly held on to the dashboard as she braked and accelerated without any warning.

She lived in the posh West End and as she drove into her driveway told me the house belonged to her ex-husband and she had got it as alimony when they split. It was a rich property by Delhi standards and I wondered what else she had milked the poor bastard for. No wonder Menon had dumped her.

Inside, the house was done up in what Delhiites like to call the nouveau riche style. What I understand is that it had thick plush carpets, wall to wall, imported furniture and a prominent bar in the drawing room. There was the usual display of crystal on the sideboard in what was the dining area of the biggish drawing room. We had hardly entered when a servant in smart white livery offered us cold water in cut glasses served on what was obviously a silver tray. On the walls hung paintings and one was M.F. Hussain's favourite one with horses. I assumed it was an original. It is the done thing to make appreciative noises and I dutifully went through the motions. Misty beamed from cheek to cheek.

'What does your husband do?' I asked.

'You mean my ex. Oh, he's in import-export,' she said.

That explains it, I told myself. But import-export was also an euphemism for smugglers of antiques, drugs and all kinds of contraband.

'What will you have to drink?' she asked.

'I thought we were going to see the Kutub,' I said.

'That can wait,' she said imperiously and waddled up to the bar to pour two large drinks from a cut glass decanter.

'Ice and soda?' she asked.

I opted for some ice and we clinked glasses and said cheers.

She guided me to a soft green leather sofa and asked me to sit while she excused herself. I sat around and looked at the various decorative items lining the built-in recesses in one wall. There was a complete set of bronze and brass nutcrackers, which looked antique but could have been made yesterday. In another recess was a complete set of leather-bound Encyclopedia Britannica. I doubted very much if any of those volumes had been ever opened by anyone but it looked neat and clean so someone must be dusting it regularly. Then there were the usual brass and copper statues of Ganesh and some other deities dwarfed by a gigantic one of Natraj. And the usual silver, supposedly old family collection.

On the coffee table were laid out some books on Delhi's monuments and the pictorial stuff about modern painting and so on. The obligatory LCD TV, and a complicated looking music system took up one corner. There were rather large blowups in ornate silver frames of Misty and a good-looking though effeminate young man, presumably her son.

All in all, a very neatly laid out drawing room. Obviously, there were no children in the house and if any did visit the room must have been out of bounds. It had the designer look and some interior decorator must have had a ball making it look like some kind of a rich man's home. Of course, he or she must have also made a lot of money. The place didn't look like anyone ever lived in it. No children, no pets, none of the wear and tear of real life. It could have been a museum or a mausoleum. A split air-conditioner announced the place was centrally air-conditioned and potted plants breathed something like perfumed air in the room. It was quite a perfect setting for Byzantine-style plotting and planning.

Misty sailed into the room from one of the heavy doors with frosted and etched glass panes and shining brass and cut glass knobs that presumably led to other rooms in the house. She had changed into a diaphanous kind of kaftan, freshened up her make-up and done all the things some women do before they begin to play the great seduction scene. I suppose she had picked up this talent from some Hollywood movie or her friends.

I leaned back in my seat and gave her an admiring look. The least I could do because I was damned if I was going to be seduced. We sipped our drinks till she asked me about me. I told her in the briefest way possible my climb down from the dizzy heights of advertising to being a writer.

'Oh, dear! That must be terrible. Living all alone and no one to look after you,' she said warming up to her seduction plan.

'Not at all! Not at all. I assure you it is quite comfortable. I have my Punditji to cook and look after me. My Doggie and a cat to keep me company. Quite comfortable, actually.'

'But you need people, you know women companions, or are you queer. I'm told most writers are like that guy Seth who also lives somewhere in the hills.'

'Is that so?' I said.

'Of course. I know for a fact that most creative people are homos. Look at all the artists and the fashion designers.'

'What do you mean for a fact?'

'Well, my son is a designer and lives with his boyfriend next door. He won't marry and says he can't stand women.'

'Nothing wrong with that. I mean, homosexuality by itself is no crime. It is a matter of personal preferences, inclinations.'

'That's what his psychiatrist says. I've given up on him. Anyway let's talk about you. And here let me refresh your drink . . . '

While she waddled off to the bar I considered my position. Life was looking quite rosy but I had to slip out before the next line of questioning began. That was bound to centre around where I was staying in Delhi and that kind of intelligence gathering, which women are rather astute at. And Menon was bound to crop up as a conversation piece. And sure enough the moment she came back she asked me where I was staying. I told her.

'Of all the people! That bastard! Do you know how badly he used to treat Leela. It's a wonder she didn't kill the fat slob.'

'Leela never told me about that,' I said pretending to be innocent of any kind of marital discord between Menon and the lately departed Leela.

'Oh! She didn't? Well, I'll tell you.' Her voice dropped to a whisper and she snuggled up close to me and said, 'He used to get her whipped by that bastard servant of his, Swami.'

Again I came up with an incredulous look, 'Izzatso?'

'Believe you me,' she said. 'The son of a bitch even buggered my son, you know. I could have killed him, I was so furious.'

'But you said your son was a homosexual . . . '

'Yes, he is but that doesn't mean you rape him,' she sputtered.

She was getting real red in the face and the whisky was doing what it did best. Make her angrier. So, there was truth in what Menon had told me about the holiday on the lake in Kashmir.

'My God! That's horrible. I didn't know Menon was that kind of a man. Where did all this happen and why didn't you report him to the police?'

'Police? You must be joking. They would have locked up my son instead. And all this happened in Kashmir. And if you know Menon you also know that he knows everybody who's anybody. What could I have done? I'm a poor woman. And then there was Leela to consider. Poor girl was forced to see all this sordid stuff.'

The next step in such a situation calls for tears. Copious outpourings from the ducts in the eyes. And boy, did it pour? Soon her eye make-up was running all over her rotund cheeks, her mighty bosom heaved with muted sobs and, in between, her eyes wide open beseeching me to lend her a shoulder or better still hold her in my arms.

I did the next best thing. I took out my handkerchief, offered it to her and excused myself to go to the toilet. I congratulated myself on having made a successful exit and now that emotions on her part were running high I could possibly get her to commit to doing what I wanted her to do.

I came out of the toilet, a very upset expression on my face and showing great concern for her predicament said, 'Surely, you can and should do something about it.'

She had stopped the tears and regained some sort of composure. So, the first thing she did was excuse herself to repair her face which she did in double quick time and was back with a fresh drink looking as if nothing had happened only minutes ago. Some women can do that very successfully. Tears one moment and laughter the next. I haven't yet been able to figure that one out.

She asked me as if she hadn't been out of the room, 'What do you think I should do?'

I knew I had her. Whatever my shortcomings, and there are many, I can be very persuasive when I want to be. It is an art one learns when selling dumb ideas to dumber clients in the advertising business. It comes in very handy when you want to motivate people to do your bidding. Of course, Menon is the master and I'm sure I picked up some of the finer points from him.

I looked pointedly at my watch and Misty asked me not to worry about the time.

'They light up the Kutub late in the evening. We'll go and see it and then I'll take you to dinner at a Thai restaurant in Mehrauli from where you also get a view of the Kutub and the surrounding area.'

Thai restaurant sounded mighty fine but these places are expensive in my experience, and unless someone is treating you or you are on an expense account it is a big no no for aspiring writers. Hoping to slip out of the dinner bit I told her I was to be at another place for dinner. She vetoed that immediately and asked me to ring up the imaginary host and cancel the invite. Besides, she told me, why was I passing off a free meal. According to her, she was entitled to complimentary food and drinks at that place for some services rendered by her in the past.

After another round of drinks she rose to go and change and asked me to make my calls and so on. I walked to the corner of the room where an imitation antique brass phone was positioned on a peg table. I had no doubt that Misty would be listening in at the extension in her room and called my ex-wife. The servant answered and I learnt she wasn't home. I felt relieved and quite casually told him to tell the memsahib that I won't be joining her for dinner. That was one successful lie. Now even if Misty looked at the dialed numbers in the telephone's memory bank she'll get a legitimate number.

We set off for the Kutub in my car and I wasn't in the least interested in seeing that old and crumbling piece of masonry. I remember reading in the papers how many school children had died in a stampede inside the monument when the lights went off. It was, like most of that area, jinxed. Somebody had lit it up with coloured spots and it all made for a rather garish display.

We didn't even bother to get out of the car and after a few minutes of staring at it in silence, Misty thought we were cutting into our drinking time by hanging around there. I couldn't have agreed more. Besides, Delhi is one of those unbelievable cities where bars shut down by eleven and restaurants have to down shutters. It is the kind of logic that only makes sense to farmers and other assorted puritans that inflict this cruelty on hard working and fun loving people.

But Delhi with all its pretensions of being a city is in reality a conglomeration of villages neatly laid out in colonies spread in an arc on the southern, eastern and western parts of the capital. The city is actually only in the area called Shahajahanabad or Old Delhi in the north. But when the events I am narrating were taking place, the city built by the Moghul Shahajahan and named after him, was fast becoming a slum with buildings crumbling, sanitation in total disarray and the majesty of its old havelis and palaces threatened by mildew, cobwebs and ruined gardens. The new rich had moved and settled in the south and as far away as possible from Old Delhi.

20

After a rather passable Thai dinner, more suitable for north Indian palates, and with Misty pointing out various personalities in the fashion world, models and designers and such, we were about to leave when her son sashayed to our table.

'What a surprise, Mother dear,' he squeaked and made a pass at her cheek.

I was introduced as a 'nice man but who for some reason is a friend of that despicable bastard Menon'. The young man was called Goldie, though I'm sure he had a perfectly decent and regular name.

'Oh, not that Menon! Leela auntie's husband? He gave me a horrible time in Kashmir, didn't he Mother?' Goldie said with an exaggerated movement of his eyebrows. Then he looked me full in the face and winked lewdly. I was dumbstruck. Sonofabitch was making a pass at me. I mouthed 'fuck off' and he gave a wicked smile and pirouetted and moved on to join some other people.

I had gone rather red under the collar of my collarless T-shirt. You know what I mean. Misty sensed my anger, discomfort and suggested we leave. That was the only sensible thing she had said that whole evening and I rose and moved off towards the exit. Behind me I heard a mocking laugh and when I looked back I could make out in the dim light that it had emanated from Goldie who while waving good-bye with one hand was suggestively rubbing his crotch with the other. It was one moment when I felt happy that Menon had buggered the little shit.

I don't care either way for queers. I have known quite a few in my time and so long as they mind their arses it doesn't bother me in the least. However, Goldie was one of the younger lot who took pride in showing off their sexual preference in public. In that he was no different from the male prostitutes one saw in the lanes and by-lanes of the Old City or in the Maidan in Calcutta or on Cuffe Parade in Bombay. While I can't put my finger on it, I find it repulsive. Love between two people of the same gender has been sanctified for thousands of years by all the great civilizations known to man. But it is only now in the twenty-first century that we have people talking of gay rights and marching down Calcutta's streets or some other city talking of empowerment and emancipation. I support their claim for a change in the law governing sexual relationships between like-minded individuals regardless of gender. I support their right to bring up babies, get married and do all the things that so-called normal people do. But I still can't put my finger on why I resent blatant displays of their sexual preferences. Perhaps, too much brain washing in my childhood.

The drive back was uneventful and I made a mental note to never visit that restaurant again. It wasn't the food or the service. That was passable as it is for most Delhi eateries. It was the ambience of the place. Everything was palpably false. The décor with those plastic flowers and shrubs imported from Bangkok, the lit up Kutub Minar, planes landing and taking off at the Delhi airport, the oddly dressed men and women pretending they were lolling around in some medieval nawab's haveli. It was what some people who know better would have described as a big scam. But then as Menon would paraphrase Barnum: Delhi is full of suckers with more being born every minute.

I dropped Misty off at her door and she gave me a more than affectionate hug and suggested a nightcap. I knew it was coming and had prepared the ground for it by mentioning en route that the food wasn't sitting quite well and my tummy was feeling very queasy and so on and so forth. You poor man, she said, and we decided to be in touch for another outing.

In the Defence Colony house the lights were on and I guessed Menon was back. He has no predictable times for coming and going. Sure enough he was sprawled out on the sofa in the drawing room and Swami was massaging his legs.

'Painting the town red, eh?' Menon said when I walked in.

'Not exactly. Don't have the appetite or the stamina for that kind of stuff,' I told him and helped myself to a glass of cognac.

'Pretty good stuff. Picked it up at Bangkok duty free only a few hours ago,' Menon informed me.

'Now that's a coincidence. I didn't know you had gone to Bangkok. I had a meal at what passes off for a Thai restaurant.'

'You had a Thai meal in New Delhi? Are you out of your mind? These fucks don't know the difference between a Thai meal and a Punjabi dhaba's chowmien,' Menon snorted derisively.

Obviously, the man knew better. After all he was coming from Bangkok.

'Anyway, where did you go and who took you?' Menon asked.

'An old friend I ran into a bookshop in CP. I don't think you know him.'

Telling Menon that there was anyone on this planet he didn't know was like showing the proverbial red rag to a bull. That is, anyone of consequence. Obviously, people who visit bookshops and take friends out to dinner at expensive Thai restaurants must be men of significance and importance.

'Nah! You can't know him,' I said to rub it in.

'Like bloody hell I don't,' he shouted and sprang to his feet and in the process kicked Swami to the floor. He paced the room some and said, 'Tell me. Now. This instant.'

Needling a man like Menon is a fine art and one must have considerable experience in this particular field.

'I can't see how you can know him,' I repeated maliciously.

Menon scowled, knocked back his cognac and poured himself another one. He was now reaching meltdown and I expected a major explosion any moment. Swami too sensed it and slid out of the room as unobtrusively as possible. I stretched my legs, crossed them at the ankles and leaned back to enjoy the show.

'Well,' he thundered, 'aren't you going to tell me?'

'Its not important,' I told him.

'That's for me to decide,' the man shouted back.

'Hey, cool it. No need to shout and wake the neighbours up.'

'I'll shout as loud as I please,' he roared. Meltdown was approaching and critical temperatures were flashing in red all over Menon's fat torso, face and his arms were about to go into the windmill mode. Boy, was he angry.

'Well, you can rave and rant as much as you like. I'm off to a good night's sleep,' I told him and went up to my room. The last I heard was the sound of breaking crystal which was without a doubt Menon flinging his glass at the wall nearest to him.

I still didn't have a workable idea and was toying around with some when I drifted off to sleep. As usual I had my quota of dreams in technicolour and widescreen. One of the joys of living all alone is the capacity to be able to dream as you will and continue your dreams like a taped film for nights on end. Sometimes just for the vicarious thrill of it I like to have nightmares. Like the one when I start flying and land up in an icy cave in the high mountains. My favourite one is travelling on a train and getting off at some unknown station and then being unable to get back on the train because it has left without me while I am negotiating a cup of tea. Because now I am in an unknown place and I've got to start from scratch. More often than not I fall in love with a village belle who has a startling resemblance to my ex-wife and go through the whole rigmarole of marriage. As usual, the dream kind of tapers off and I am back on some other train hurtling through the darkness of the night to an unknown destination to begin with my story all over again.

The other one that I always have is about being shipwrecked. Then like Robinson Crusoe I go about building a whole new world where life is a bed of roses, fresh coconut milk laced with gin (the gin always appears mysteriously), dozens of girl-fridays lounging around with nothing on except fig leafs in case some unexpected visitors drop in on our island paradise. Then when life gets too good I manage to spy a ship out of the horizon and wave for it to go away but the people on it get all wrong and land up on my beach to rescue me. I am taken away dragging and screaming with the wails of my nubile wenches ringing in my ears. That night none of these dreams made a start and I contended myself with one hazy black and white about some ghost or the other.

The next day as I sat in the lawn sipping the excellent coffee prepared by Swami I saw Menon hurrying out of the house. His driver followed him lugging a heavy briefcase. He didn't bother to look in my direction and I am sure the bugger was still pissed off with me from last night. He's a spiteful bastard when he wants to be which is most of the time.

I delved further into my copy of the *Times* that as usual was full of all kinds of uninteresting news, at least to me. I glanced at the entertainment section and saw something that could be worth my time. An exhibition of paintings at one of the galleries. I have found that there are two ways to pass your time without spending a penny. One is to hang around bookshops that are mercifully air-conditioned these days and the other is to pop into a gallery, air-conditioned, and pose as a potential buyer. When one gets bored with all this then one can walk into the lobby of any five-star hotel and make oneself rather comfortable in the plush sofas meant for visitors, merge with guests waiting for someone or about to check out. There is always something worthwhile going in a hotel lobby and with flight crews checking in or out on a regular basis one can ogle at all the beautiful airhostesses except the ones from some American airlines. They are invariably old hags.

But before I could decide on how to spend my day Swami told me that there was a call for me. The chances were it was my ex-wife or Misty. I don't think anyone else knew about my visit except for some cronies at the Press Club. And sure enough it was Misty.

She wanted to know how I was placed for the day and I said I was tied up with a lunch meeting (all lies) but had nothing lined up for the evening. How about dinner? I said that wouldn't be possible though I could pop in for drink before going on my dinner date. Again lies. It was agreed that I would have a sundowner with her at her place.

It was that evening that the germ of an idea was born. I had finished my first drink and Misty was busy fussing around making me a second one when she said, 'Did you ever see Leela on stage?'

'No. I didn't know her then,' I told her.

'She was quite a rave in Bombay in those days and she also acted in Calcutta.'

'Well, she does have all the makings of a histrionic personality. I'm sure she must have been a very good actress. What a pity I missed her,' I said. I had nearly started talking about her in the past tense but the old presence of mind worked and I didn't make that mistake.

'Well, not really. I have her on tape and you can see her.'

'You mean you have a video, really?'

'You bet. I have always been a great fan of hers and when she was on the stage I would have all her plays recorded because most times I couldn't make it to her performances in Bombay or Calcutta. I have, I think ten or is it eleven, videos of her.'

I showed great enthusiasm and jumped out of my sofa and asked if I could see them.

'Well, you could but you would have to stay the night to see all of them,' she said and winked. It was one of those kind of winks that suggested a steamy night tucked into bed with the VCR going full speed ahead in between hectic bouts of lovemaking.

That was a no. No as far as I was concerned. But I needed to see the tapes.

'I would love to stay awake the whole night to see them but I'm unfortunately tied up in the evenings with my editor and publisher discussing my manuscript and so on. It is really a pity. But you wouldn't mind lending them to me, would you?'

She hummed and hawed and said that she never let them out of her sight because she only had the master copies and knowing how people were careless with other people's tapes never lent them. I gently persuaded her to lend them to me and promised to return them to her in a pristine condition. Since that promise wasn't cutting much ice with her I went a step forward and agreed to spend a night at her house going over the tapes and discussing Leela's performances.

'Promise?' she said.

I did the usual hope-to-die routine and she went and gave me the tapes and made me seal my promise with a rather long and wet kiss. I managed to act my way out of that and even gave her tits a gentle squeeze as an advance payment for things to come. And then with all the silkiness at my command made my exit with some more wet smooches and squeezing of rotund bums.

I watched the tapes that night in Menon's house. It was a scary experience hearing Leela's voice on those tapes and I almost felt she was sitting right next to me when I knew fully well she was six-foot deep in the drawing room floor. I had told Swami to leave some sardine sandwiches for me and I did not need him for the night. Menon was god-only-knows where and I had the whole house to myself.

They were rather high quality tapes and well preserved. I listened and watched them till I saw dawn break and heard the birds actively chirping in the bushes in the lawn. I stopped the machine, picked up the tapes and with my eyes nearly popping out of their sockets managed to make it to my room and crawl into my bed. I think I slept till well after lunch and when I came down for a wake-me-up coffee Swami unwittingly gave me an idea that I knew I could use to my advantage and get out of Menon's clutches.

As I sipped my coffee Swami came up to me and said he thought he heard voices in the night. I told him it was some tapes I was watching.

'No. Saar,' he told me. 'It was Leela mem. I swear.'

'Come on Swami. You and I know she's dead and buried. Surely, you don't believe in ghosts?'

'But I do, saar. I have heard and seen so many in my life. I'm sure it was the Mem's ghost.'

I tut-tuted some more and shooed him off pretending I was

more interested in the news. But in actual fact this was where the germ of an idea was sown. My brain was whirling like one of Rumi's dervishes and I knew I had hit the jackpot. However, the first thing was to get those tapes copied without anyone knowing about their existence. I dressed hastily and asked Swami to call the car that had been put at my disposal by the ever-generous Menon and without waiting for lunch I took off. I told Swami I had some urgent work and I would be back later in the day.

I told the driver to take me to a studio in the Okhla industrial area that I had used for post-production work in the old days. I knew the owner and asked him to let me use one of his video suites for transferring some material. He said I was lucky because there was one available right away as the man who had booked it hadn't turned up. He also put a young editor at my disposal and I explained to him what I wanted and the man ran off copies of all the tapes and then burnt them on a CD.

I knew I was fighting a monster and remembered vaguely something Nietzsche had written in *Beyond Good and Evil*. If I recollect it went something like this: He who fights monsters should be careful lest he thereby becomes a monster. And if thou gaze into the abyss, the abyss will also gaze unto you. I think this was also a recurring theme in a lot of Hollywood movies where good eventually triumphs over evil but not before the do-gooder himself is on the brink of becoming evil.

I often hear people discuss American foreign policy in these terms specially the invasion of Iraq and George W. Bush's talk of an axis of evil. In my case there was only one villain in my life and that was Menon. I had to get rid of him, get exorcised, as it were. And then ride off into the sunset. Like in any good Western.

What Swami had told me about ghosts jolted memories of the days when Menon and I shared a flat on Sudder Street in Calcutta. I would often find Menon talking about strange visitations to his room, shadow-like figures moving around his bed and colourful flashing lights. I used to make fun of him in those days and call him an old maid and names like that. But that didn't deter him and one day he announced he was moving out to some other place in the lakes area.

'Can't live with these blasted ghosts of English men and their women,' was his argument.

Perhaps, there was a kernel of truth in what he said. The

chowkidar had once told me a story about the original owners of the mansion before it was bought by some Indian and converted into flats. He had said that the Englishman who owned the building was a burra sahab who in a fit of jealousy had killed his memsahib when he found her in bed with someone else. After that he had shot himself and ever since that night people used to hear sounds of quarrels followed by gunshots and screams and so on. I asked him if he had seen anything himself but he said he believed in the Hanuman Chalisa and that kept all kinds of evil spirits away from him. I had told Menon that but in his inimitable style he had disregarded that bit of advice and called Hanuman, the monkey god, a figment of a demented imagination, a character from the original science fiction called the Ramayana and such derogatory stuff. He had then packed his bags and moved on to the new place.

I stayed behind in Sudder Street because it was close to the office and my favourite pub on Park Street. I took on another colleague as a partner to share the flat's rent. But Menon and I met in office on a daily basis and invariably landed up at the Park Street pub for a lunchtime drink or sometimes in the evening. The additional charm of living on in Sudder Street was that on the top floor of the mansion was a flat which housed some rather good-looking whores and whose services we used whenever we felt the need. Menon was also a regular punter and whoremaster but he never stayed the night because of what he called 'evil spirits'. So, in a way you could say the man was scared of something even if it was so nebulous as ghosts.

The plan shaping up in my mind was to edit the CDs carefully and keep Leela's dialogues from the various plays in a sort of order so that when the doctored CDs were played the listener would be convinced that Leela was talking to him. In this case Menon. Most of the plays were those mystery plays made famous by Agatha Christie and in one of them there was Leela telling someone in a rather ominous voice: I know where you were last night. Taken out of context most of those dialogues could make for excellent tools to spook Menon.

Of course, I was taking it for granted that Menon was

'spookable'. As a trial run I waited for Menon to be at home and in what passed for his relaxed moods. The opportunity came earlier than I expected because he had picked himself up another woman, one of those trying to get into some modeling assignment with Menon's company and was doing it the simple and easy way. By lying back and enjoying it or pretending to enjoy it. No sweat, pal.

When she walked in and he introduced her I realized it was time to make my move. After a decent interval, a drink or two, I excused myself on the pretext that I had something to do and walked out of the drawing room. I had bought myself a mobile phone and I used it to ring the phone sitting on a small table right next to Menon's drink.

Generally, he never answered the phone himself. That was Swami's job. But when he had a female visitor Swami would disappear somewhere on the terrace of the house and away from the phone in the hallway or the extension in the kitchen.

I had cued the CD on its player and the moment Menon answered I played it. Leela's voice floated eerily through the mobile phone and to Menon's ear. It was the one where she had said: I know where you were last night. On the other end I heard Menon gasp and say: What? It was one of the expected responses from a man who had murdered his wife and buried her in his drawing room. I had doctored the CD so he could hear Leela repeating what she had said. I then switched off the mobile.

After sometime I walked into the drawing room looking for a refill. In actuality I wanted to see the reaction on Menon's face. He was reacting all right. The bimbo had been told to bugger off. He was pacing the room and muttering to himself. Swami had been summoned and was standing and shaking in one corner. As I watched the scene I knew I had hit the jackpot.

Menon saw me at the bar and said, 'Do you know what happened just now?'

'What?' I deadpanned.

'I had a call. And it was that damned Leela.'

'What? But you told me she was dead and buried six feet under!' I exclaimed.

Menon fixed his beady eyes on me and said, 'That's the point. She was calling from the grave, I swear.'

'What rot! Surely you don't believe in all that stuff about ghosts?'

Swami piped in, almost on cue, 'I also heard Leela mem, saar.'

'There. Now Swami is also hearing things. Can't you believe me when I tell you what I heard,' Menon screamed.

The man was fast approaching hysteria and I knew how to spur him on.

'Look Menon. You are an aging old fart. Ghosts and all that is very well for little boys. Wake up man. This is the twenty-first century and there are no ghosts.'

'Like bloody hell there aren't. Look, I swear on my dead mother that it was Leela's voice.'

Getting Menon swear to anything on his dead mother was the closest you could get to know that the man was telling the truth or at least was telling the world that what he was saying was true.

'Okay. Just for argument's sake I agree to the fact that there was a phone call and the voice on the other end was Leela's. But how has Leela's so-called ghost got hold of a telephone?'

'Why? Ghosts can get anything. Don't you know?'

I gave him one of my half-and-half snorts that said in many ways that he was talking through his arsehole. That, Menon didn't take kindly to. He exploded and in his fashion he smashed his whisky glass against the nearest wall. Menon was getting to be predictable. In that he wasn't much different from most of us. He paced around the room some more. I sat back on a sofa and pretended to be totally relaxed, waiting for the next act.

A friendly electronics expert had armed me with a remote that he claimed worked the CD player from a distance of at least a 100 metres. It could also activate Menon's phone from my mobile. I had the gadget in my trouser pocket and sitting around looking calm and cool pressed the right buttons. I am no good with technological innovations but this was one gadget I had mastered ever since I had launched my plan to spook Menon. Sure enough, the phone rang. Menon looked at it if it was a venomous snake. Then in a quavering voice asked me if I could answer it.

I picked up the phone and there was Leela's voice at the other end, loud and clear. It made both Swami and Menon's eyes pop. I pretended I was shocked and dropped the receiver.

'God! What was that?' I gasped.

The phone went dead and the dialtone came back as I bent and picked it up gingerly and replaced it on its cradle. In the stunned silence I made myself walk to the bar and with visibly shaking hands poured myself a drink and sloshed some of it outside the glass. I drank it down in one gulp and again said, 'God dammit!'

My thespian exposure was limited to being a tree in a school play. I knew I wouldn't be able to ham it any further and pretending that I was going to be sick bolted from the room, up the stairs and into my room. For a while I stood there holding my stomach and heaving with laughter. This was the best I had ever got out of that old sod. Here was the brain behind the most successful advertising company spooked by a childish prank. I knew it was the kind of story that would have kept me in free dinners for a lifetime. At least in the circles where Menon had made most of his enemies. It was too much. I gloated on the prospect ahead, for a while, and then slipped into bed and drifted off into a rather dreamless sleep.

I woke with the first light and to the excited chirping of the tits in Menon's back garden. The cat was back in action and the birds were in their usual state of panic. Morning bus services rumbled down the main road and the neighbours were getting their cars warmed up as they set off for their morning walk.

That's not as strange as it sounds. In New Delhi people go for walks in their cars. It is one hell of a funny place because most of the colonies seem to have lost their public parks to parking lots, drug peddlers and prostitutes. The denizens of this grotesque urban sprawl then have to drive to the nearest public park, usually the tomb of some dead Sultan or emperor. These parks and the monuments inside them tell the tale of a bygone era of opulence and are protected from vandals and such by the Archeological Survey of India, a bonus from our English masters.

The area encompassed by these tombs is neatly landscaped with walking paths and well-maintained gardens. The good tax payers of Defence Colony, not Menon and his ilk, but retired army and government officials and their health conscious offsprings, women gone fat after repeated childbirth and now wanting to regain their lost figures and other people wanting to show off the latest in walking shoes and track suits, haunt a patch of green called the Lodhi Gardens. Here, they are joined by others from the various assorted colonies in the vicinity who have also driven up in their cars for their constitutionals. The late risers or early office goers catch up with the routine in the evenings when the sun has run its course and a mild breeze makes a walk worthwhile.

Since the colonies around the Lodhi Gardens are populated by the upmarket or to put it more bluntly the movers and shakers crowd made up of senior bureaucrats, politicians, lobbyists and entrepreneurs of various hues and the occasional diplomat tired of his or her gym in the air-conditioned basement, there is an air of importance attached to these morning and evening rituals. Most breakfast conversations in these homes are generally dominated by talk of who was in the park with whom. And evening cocktails are sprinkled with mild doses of name-dropping.

I brushed my teeth and set off down the stairs to get a cup of coffee. The usual rich fragrance of the brew was missing because the kitchen fires had not been lit by Swami. He was sitting at the feet of his master his head buried in his arms while his master sat upright staring dead ahead like he had been pole-axed. It was the same scene I had left to disappear upstairs the night before. It appeared nothing had changed except for the light. The drawing room lights were on but they were looking faded as the morning sun was blazing through the big plate glass windows. It was something you see in a play when the audience is being told that night had passed into day and it is now Scene Two of Act I.

In a manner of speaking it was Scene Two in the drawing room of Menon's mansion. Enter right was me, tousled hair and all. I walked up to Swami and touched him on the shoulder. Swami shot upright as I if had hit him with an electric prod.

'Coffee,' I told him.

Swami walked towards the kitchen like a somnambulist. I heard him filling the percolator and then he let the water run in the sink and probably washed his face. I shook Menon by his shoulder and he too sprang awake. His eyes focused on me and blinked. I knew the bugger was alive and asked him what he was doing sleeping on the sofa with his eyes open.

He looked around at the familiar layout and watched me go around switching off the lights.

He squinted as the bright morning light hit him and muttered, 'It is morning then?'

'Rise and shine, kiddo,' I told him.

'Stop that schoolboy shit,' Menon growled.

He wasn't in the best of moods. He never was when he woke up. Most times you wouldn't get a word out of him until he had had his first couple of cups of coffee. He looked balefully around the room and then with great effort got to his feet and waddled off towards his room.

I had read somewhere, probably in some book on torture, that don't let the victim sleep. Apparently sleep deprivation is a favourite tool for third degree treatment in police lock ups worldwide. As such I was ready with my next devious attack.

In the various CDs I had of Leela's voice there was one from a poetry recital where she had read poems by the Sufi mystic Rumi. Sufism had hit the rich and famous in those days with Usha Uthup singing songs like 'mast kalandar' at the Trincas restaurant in Calcutta's Park Street. Since the rich and famous did not understand a word of Persian or Urdu they had to make do with transliterations of Rumi's poems by English and German writers. One of Rumi's poems that I found particularly suited for the ongoing torture of Menon was described as a love song and it went like this:

Come, come, whoever you are.
Wonderer, worshipper, lover of leaving.
It doesn't matter.
Ours is not a caravan of despair.
Come, even if you have broken your vow
A thousand times.
Come, yet again, come, come.

Love poem or not it had a particularly ghoulish ring to it when taken in the context of the dead Leela's position six feet under Menon's drawing room. This was as good a time as any to play it. I knew that Menon, a creature of habit, always carried his mobile phone to the loo. From there ensconced on his throne he would make calls all over the place. He always maintained that his best ideas came when he was sitting on the crapper. This exercise could last for the better part of an hour. But I was going to put an end to it. And how!

Swami gave me my mug of coffee and I gleefully trotted up the stairs to my room. I rang Menon on his mobile and as luck would have it got him on the first try. Then I put on the CD and as Leela's voice drifted through the ether into Menon's hairy ears the lyrics took on a frightening and ominous meaning.

'Come, come whoever you are' found Menon on his feet and by the time 'come, even if you have broken your vow' drifted into his consciousness he was out of the loo, stark naked and shouting for Swami. The moment the poem finished I switched off my phone and came downstairs and calmly asked the naked Menon and a trembling Swami what all the shouting was about.

Menon was standing in the middle of the drawing room, atop Leela's grave and stamping on it. He had driven himself into a frenzy and quite forgotten that he was buck naked. He had left his lungi in the loo and as he stomped around his belly bounced in all directions and his pathetic limp prick swung around like a pendulum. It was a sight that made me want to laugh and I was laughing inwardly. And the memory of it keeps me in splits even today.

'Hey! Stop it!' I commanded.

But Menon was too far gone and he was now telling the ground beneath his feet that he was 'coming. I'm coming to get you, you bitch'. His voice had picked up a rhythm of its own and like a child reciting a nursery rhyme he paraphrased good old Rumi and repeated himself ad infinitum. I am sure that the place where the good poet was buried must have received a severe churning that day. Eventually, Menon ran out of steam and collapsed on his favourite sofa and hurled the phone that went flying and smashed against the wall precisely at the place where his whisky glass had landed the other night. This Menon was perfecting the art of throwing all kinds of missiles.

Swami went and brought his lungi for him and draped it across his lap like a blanket. His nudity was covered for the moment and the man seeing that seemed to be regaining his sense of dignity. His breathing became normal and he held his face in his hands.

'What was all that about?' I asked him gently.

Menon dropped his hands and looked at me, his eyes lost and forlorn. Then a tear trickled down one cheek followed in rapid succession by several and Menon the hulk was crying unabashedly. His body shook as he drew long breaths and let them out like elephants do when they are wallowing in a river.

'Come on, old man. It can't be all that bad,' I said in the most sympathetic tone I could muster. At the rate I was going I could jolly well audition for a play or film, I told myself.

Menon sniffed, wiped his tears from his cheeks with a corner of his lungi and asked for a drink. Swami had seen it coming and he was on to it like a flash. The amber fluid disappeared down his throat in a twinkling and he signaled for a refill.

The second drink worked wonders for him and he cleared his throat and said, 'Don't ever use the word quote unquote "come" in front of me, ever again, or I'll kill you.'

'Kill me? What for?' I said.

'For saying *come*,' Menon repeated.

'Now what's wrong with saying *come*,' I went on innocently.

Menon charged out of his sofa and had me by my throat. Fat as he was the bugger was quite strong and could have easily suffocated me if it hadn't been for Swami who broke his grip on my throat and led him back to the sofa. He seated him and draped his lungi across his lap.

I now had him where I wanted. He was terrified, if that is the word. Frightened people do all kinds of silly things. I looked at him from a distance and wondered what drove men like him who could kill without batting an eyelid and then lose their wits at the mere suggestion of a non-existent entity like a ghost. Perhaps, Hamlet had it right when he told Horatio: 'There are more things in heaven and earth, than are dreamt of in your philosophy ...'

23

I didn't know much about Menon's business except that he was doing quite well and I mean mega-bucks well. He had a plush office somewhere in the malls of Gurgaon, the satellite town that had sprouted almost overnight around New Delhi. I assumed that he was headed there when he left the house later in the morning. I had got quite used to his abrupt departures and arrivals and his habit of never telling me or anyone else where he was going.

I enjoyed a leisurely breakfast of ham and eggs chased with some excellent coffee that, Swami informed me, was imported. The morning papers had the usual stuff about another rape and how Delhi was fast becoming the rape capital of the country. Apparently some diplomat had been forced into a car after she came out of an auditorium where foreign films were being screened. She was then driven off to a lonely spot and raped by a man she couldn't identify. The paper said the police had an identikit description of him and expected to nab the culprit soon. But then I had read that before. The culprits invariably seemed to get away and I knew that the diplomat was going to be just another statistic. Well, what can you expect in a city where people flock to from all over the country and learn to mind their business and look after their own skins.

Swami cleared the breakfast plate and without much ado asked me what I thought about this business of Leela mem's voice. Like his master he too was one spooked man. I told him the truth because I knew he would never believe it. I said it looked like someone was playing a big practical joke. Of course, that someone also knew that he and his master had killed the woman and buried her in the drawing room. Doesn't look too good to me, I told him.

Swami was a sharp thinker. While he was frightened of Leela's ghost he was more frightened of finding himself hanging from one end of a rope in Delhi's Tihar jail. I could see in his eyes what he was thinking. And his thought process was running somewhat like this: Okay. It is a practical joke. But the prankster, whoever he or she is, knows about the murder. Right now only I, the master and this writer fellah know. So, who is this other person?

I knew he would be nagged by this thought for the better part of his life. I didn't know then how horribly wrong I was.

In his experience people who know other people's dark secrets always end up blackmailing them. He would automatically rule out a man like me because he knew I was already on Menon's payroll. I also suspected he thought me too principled or weak-kneed to go in for blackmail. He had to be steered in a direction where he would convince himself that he knew the identity of the prankster and do something about it. And once he was convinced he would take only one kind of action. Murder. It was the easiest way out for a man like him. He had done it before and was no stranger to the business of killing other people. One more murder wouldn't make any difference to his general health and on top of that save him from going to the gallows. I had Swami where I wanted him and Menon too.

Now that Menon was spooked I wanted to give him some time before launching the second part of my plan. But he did that for me unknowingly. From what I learnt later he had the advertising account for a famous brand of coffee. The slogan to promote the brand went something like: 'come alive! come alive!' He had coined this rather catchy phrase to promote the brand and it had done wonders for the sale of the coffee. In return he had raked in a substantial amount of moolah. So far, so good.

On that fateful day, with his nerves shot to hell, he charged into his Gurgaon office and called an immediate meeting of his think-tank. This meant video conferencing with his minions in various cities. In a terse command he said he wanted the slogan 'come alive, come alive' to be dropped from all advertising copy, jingles, film and what have you. And in that one broad stroke he chopped off his financial legs. He had sounded the death knell for his company. His employees sensed that something was seriously wrong with Menon and there were dark mutterings about him becoming another burnt out case, a phenomenon quite common in the advertising world.

Of course, no one knew the real reason why Menon did what he did. But then in most cases no one ever knew why Menon did what he did. And having made his pronouncement and thrown his employees into a tizzy Menon proceeded to get drunk.

There are certain areas where some of us like to believe that we are undisputed experts. One of them is human nature. There's no telling what makes the human brain tick though men and women like Sigmund Freud and his clones have written mighty fine theories on the subject. For instance, Menon was one of a kind. He was unclonable, if a word like that exists. As someone at a party once said: God must have broken the mould after creating Menon.

That evening when Menon came home, several sheets to the wind I may add, he went about berating Swami in what were definitely choice Malayalam expletives. I don't know the language but I could judge from the tone and the pitch that Swami's ancestors, mother and father, siblings and who ever else was even a distant kin were at the receiving end. The man was spitting like an angry snake and from time to time punctuated his outburst by smashing his whisky glass or any one of the expensive cut glass objets d'art against the drawing room wall. I feared for the expensive flat screen TV and the brand new, hi-tech music system.

When he had run out of steam and collapsed on his favourite sofa his beady eyes focused on me sitting quietly in one corner. His breathing steadied and he seemed to remember his manners. He shouted for Swami to give me a drink. After a long pause he mumbled something about the two of us having a talk. I nodded and shrugged as nonchalantly as I could. The last few days here had made me into quite an accomplished actor. When you are living a lie it is best to play it to the hilt. No percentage in being caught out.

'So, looks like another bad day in the office, eh?' I said to get the ball rolling.

'You can say that again. Ever since that bitch died nothing is going right,' Menon growled.

'If you are referring to Leela then you mean ever since you killed her, don't you?'

'If you insist. Of course, I killed her. She wasn't Leela any more.'

'What do you mean she wasn't Leela anymore?'

'That's what I meant. She was a *he*, you dumbass?'

'Look Menon. I may be dumb but I am not that dumb. I know a woman when I see one.'

Swami discreetly cleared his throat as if he wanted to say something. Menon glared at him and asked him to speak up.

Swami said, 'Leela mem had become a sahab, saar.'

'Now what's that supposed to mean?' I asked.

'She . . . I mean he began to wear men's clothes,' Swami managed to say.

'So she was wearing pants. What's new about that? She did fancy wearing jeans and trousers. She often wore a business woman's suit.'

'No. No,' Menon interrupted. 'She had become a man. Beard and moustache. She shaved every morning. She had a real penis and she pissed standing up straight.'

As I said, I had thought that I had heard it all. But this was something totally new. I mean I knew about sex change and all that. I had read about men becoming women and women having operations to become men. Like that guy who was a doorman at one of Delhi's posh hotels. But Leela? A man? Incredulous! I rose to my feet and looked Menon in his eyes and said, 'Have you lost your fuckin' mind?'

'No, my friend. I thought I had lost it when I first saw it. And it happened in your blasted cottage. You remember the day Leela was dancing naked in the rain on your lawn and the lightning struck close by and she fainted.'

Of course, I remembered. In my diary I have described it as the day of the thunderclap. I had carried Leela inside and summoned the doctor. Menon, as usual, was hoping she had died and was rather disappointed when she hadn't. Those were rather vivid memories.

Menon after a suitable pause began again. 'You recollect she asked for me and I went to her room. Now you better believe me. When I walked in she was lying under the quilt covered all the way up to her nose. She asked if it was me. I pulled up a chair and in my best bed-side manners asked her how she was feeling. She didn't say anything but whipped off the quilt, took my hand and placed it on her cunt. But there was no cunt there. Instead there was an erect penis and hard and round testicles.'

He paused again to let the fact sink in. I looked at him in disbelief. Surely the man was stark raving mad. Leela with a prick? Must be the booze.

'I think you were hallucinating,' I told him.

'No! I swear by my mother. Leela had grown a prick and it was thicker, harder and bigger than mine.'

Most times I took most of Menon's utterances with large dollops of salt. The bugger could lie and lie till the cows came home. But this was getting serious, specially after he swore by his mother. I think I've mentioned it earlier but I think you should be reminded that the only thing he took seriously and with almost a religious frenzy was the memory of his dead mother.

'Then ...,' I asked.

'Then what? She said she was going to bugger me. Her voice was manly and her, or rather, his grip on my hand vice-like. I panicked and fell off the chair. As I lay on the floor he sprang out of bed and pissed all over me.'

'And then ...'

'Standing up. From his brand new prick. Don't you know anything?' Menon said angrily.

I remembered the look on Menon's face as he came out of Leela's room. At that time it appeared as if he had seen an apparition of sorts. I mean the man had looked shell-shocked and I was afraid the bugger was going to croak from a heart attack or a stroke or something.

Standing behind him Swami's eyes widened in what was

palpably fear. Mine looked on in disbelief and I believe my jaw was rather hanging slackly. Or slackly hanging. This was something.

Menon snorted and signaled for a refill. Swami went about the job double quick and I too felt a need for another slug of whisky. If the matter had not been so serious it could have been hilarious and possibly kept me in free dinners for many a night. I could see why Menon got spooked so easily. Wouldn't you? I mean he had seen his ex-wife felled by lightning and soon after that seen her change her sex. Bloody hell!

Menon was getting into the stride of things.

'On my return to Delhi I rang up a doctor friend. When we met I told him of what had happened to Leela. He said that was quite common now. Gender dysphoria, he called it. A lot of women were going in for a sex change operation because they felt they were born in the wrong body or they resented male domination, the doc told me. By the way, he also said that the lightning had nothing to do with it. Leela, according to him, had had a sex change operation probably in Bangkok because that is where it was the cheapest.'

He paused, sighed and sipped his drink. Then he took another deep breath and said, 'This business is called metoidioplasty. Phallic clitoral enlargement, you understand?'

I did and I didn't. My mind went back to the day Leela had danced naked in the lawn. I tried to remember if she was a he before the thunderclap. Possibly, I had missed it all because I was watching her from a distance and the windowpanes were misted up because of the rain. Then another possibility crossed my mind. Menon could be bullshitting me. It was a distinct possibility, knowing the bugger. But then what about the tantrik and her coupling with him? The questions came in rapid succession and I had no real answers. The matter was getting surreal. If what Menon had said was true then I needed to know why Leela had undergone the sex change operation. I asked Menon if he had any ideas on that. He had plenty.

I decided to pay a visit to Leela's flat along with Mishti who had a duplicate key. She had asked me to call her Mishti instead of Misty. It's kind of cute, she had said. When we walked in it was obvious that the flat had not been used for weeks if not months. The fine sand that blows in from the Rajasthan desert every Delhi summer had coated the furniture and the carpets. A fine layer of it lay over the marble floor and it made a crunching noise under my shoes as I walked across the drawing room towards the bedroom. The bed had been made many mornings ago and everything looked to be in place which one would expect from a woman's bedroom. In the bathroom nothing had been disturbed. Towels were neatly in place but in the cabinet above the sink were the usual shaving things associated with men, aftershave bottles, a bottle of aspirin, one of fruit salt powder, another containing some tablets, toothbrush and toothpaste and a small box containing the first-aid stuff. The built-in cupboard in the bedroom was not locked and when I opened one door I could see several business suits hanging neatly. Shirts were in one shelf and men's underclothes on another. All rather expensive men's wear, I could make out from the labels. A neat row of shoes were placed in the bottom shelf.

Mishti had been watching all this in silence with her jaw hanging in disbelief. Earlier, when I had asked her if she could take me to Leela's flat she had wanted to know why and all I had told her was that I needed to pick up a book I had lent her some months back when she had come to my cottage in the hills. That was when she had told me that she had a duplicate key that Leela had kept with her in case she lost the original. Initially, she wasn't too keen on my being allowed inside in Leela's absence but with a little persuasion and hints of some serious dalliance in bed she agreed but with a warning that I wasn't to touch any of her other things.

Now she looked around and took in the dust on the mirror, the floor, the bed cover and curtains and said, 'Oh, my God.'

'Yes,' I said, 'Oh, my God.'

Irritated by my parroting her she said sharply, 'What is that supposed to mean?'

'Exactly that! This is a real mystery. Looks like there was a man living here. I wonder where her clothes are?' I said.

'A man? But how, . . . or who?' Mishti said.

'Leela would know best. Obviously, if you don't know then nobody does.'

Mishti, visibly shaken by the import of what I had said began to look around for any signs of Leela's jewellery, perfumes, lingerie and things that most women keep around the house. There was nothing to prove that a woman had ever lived there. It was a small flat, the kind you would expect to find single men or women using in any modern urban sprawl. It had a kitchenette with usual pots and pans, some dry rations. Eggs in the fridge and some ready-to-cook TV dinners. In the drawing room there was a bookcase and I picked up a book at random and told Mishti that I had got what I wanted and we could leave. But Mishti wasn't in any hurry. Her curiosity was getting the better of her and she wanted to, as she said, get to the bottom of things.

The mystery man living in the flat was something Mishti had to know all about. She went through the bedroom once again, looking under the covers, lifting the mattress. Then a quick peep under the bed as if expecting to find the mystery man. All that exertion was too much for her and finally tired she sat down on a sofa in the drawing room. I hadn't put the ceiling fan on because I knew it would raise a small dust storm and all the bending and stretching in the hot and airless flat had made Mishti sweat like an over-ridden mare. I found some glasses in a cabinet, rinsed one of them and took out a bottle of water from the fridge. I offered her a glass and she tasted a sip and thought the water was foul. I thought as much and so opened a bottle of beer. In the bar cabinet there was an assortment of alcohol but a beer, cold as it was, came in real handy at that time.

Mishti wiping the perspiration from her face with one end of her sari said, 'If I didn't know better I would bet that we were in the wrong place.'

'Looks like the flat is Leela's. After all those are her books. There is the normal collection of booze. And it also looks like she left it for a brief while, maybe for a quick weekend or something and didn't return.'

'It is her flat all right. See that painting over there. I gave it to her on her birthday. But what happened to all her lovely clothes?' Mishti was confused.

It wasn't the right time to tell her what I already knew. I mean about Leela's sex change operation. I wanted to wait and draw her out and see if she knew anything about it. I had to double-check Menon's version of things. A sex change operation by itself was no big deal. But what I knew of Leela, it did sound improbable. If there was a woman with all the feminine traits then it was her. It, therefore, followed that if she had undergone one then she must have had a solid reason. But what could that be?

'Any idea where Leela's been in the last few months?' I asked.

'She was abroad. I think Bangkok or was it the States? She came back and then took off for the hills. To your cottage, I understand. All she said was that she was going to cook Moron Menon's goose.'

'She did that all right,' I said and swigged the beer.

'How? Do tell me.' the ever curious Mishti pleaded.

'Well, for one she frightened the hell out of him.'

'Really? How nice. Well, what did she do?'

I thought about answering that question. My mind said one thing and my heart another. It was one of those secrets that explode like a bomb when exposed. Spontaneous combustion, I think it is called. She begged some more and I got out of that one by telling her it was time we left and the matter could wait for another time. Leave we did. The flat was getting to be too much. I had goose bumps when I thought of Leela's ghost looking down at us.

As we walked out of the building, Mishti said something about reporting the matter to the police. I nodded in my best absent-minded way. There was no way I was going anywhere near the police. I hated Menon for what he had done and now I hated him more for what he had made Leela do when she was alive. The very idea of Leela wanting to bugger that fat bastard and going all the way to do that by having a sex change was mind-boggling. She must have really hated him. I had heard of a case where a woman became a man in order to get a share of her father's property. But to change one's sex for the express purpose of sodomizing a man you hated – that defied my imagination. Murder may have seemed too easy a way out for her. But then as they say a woman scorned . . .

In the car Mishti went on about the mystery man in Leela's flat. What intrigued her, obviously, was what had happened to Leela's wardrobe and jewellery. Women care about such things, I've noticed. I listened in silence because there was nothing I could tell her. I had to pretend that I did not know that Leela was dead and buried.

Back in her house she demanded her pound of flesh but I was too far gone to even raise a few ounces. I pleaded a headache and postponed the matter for another time. I could see that she was getting quite pissed off with me and was a shade short of calling me all kinds of names which women reserve for impotent men. Men take sexual rejection in many ways. Some loose their temper. Some go and get drunk. And then men like me don't care either way. But women take such matters to heart. They get knotted up in their heads and stomach and become potential time bombs. It is best for the offending male to step aside or if he has any real sense to make a run for it. I like to credit myself with some sense and thought it best to fade away. So, when I asked her to call for a taxi she did it with a vengeance, most of it taken out on the telephone. You know, stuff like banging the receiver hard and shouting at the taxi operator. Then she stormed off into her bedroom and slammed the door behind her. I tiptoed out and thanked my lucky stars for the chance to escape.

In the corporate world, I had learnt, success thrives on success as much as an avalanche feeds on itself and becomes bigger and bigger as it roars down the mountainside. But when things start to go wrong they do so in the same manner as an avalanche seen in a rewind mode. By withdrawing the money making slogan which he had, in the first place, plagiarized from Rumi's poem, and putting in a tame substitute, Menon had set in motion an irreversible slide into failure. His colleagues and underlings were too scared of him to suggest a change of course. They watched in silence as the client withdrew the contract. Then they very smartly and gleefully started job hunting elsewhere taking their accounts with them.

'The rats are abandoning the sinking ship,' he informed me one evening a week after I had spooked him with come, come . . .

'What rats? Which ship?' I inquired.

'Mine, you idiot!' he barked.

'You deserve it,' I said maliciously.

'I deserve it. Is it? Et tu, you bastard,' Menon roared.

'Up yours,' I shouted back.

The idea was to keep him in a bad temper for as long as possible. His nerves, already shot to hell with all the booze he had had over the years, were now ready to give him a serious breakdown. His empire was about to collapse because nobody in the market trusted his judgement anymore.

The word was out that Menon had gone bananas. What hurt him most was that the people who were twisting the dagger into his very guts were the same people who he had uplifted and made rich. They were spreading rumours, the bankers were reacting by stopping overdrafts and the creditors were lining up outside his office. This was the ultimate nightmare for any businessman, specially a man like Menon who was fast losing whatever vestige of sanity at his command.

I should have felt sorry for him but I didn't. In my mind the man was a murderer and that too of his wife. So what if they were divorced. After all she had been the mother of his child. And she had not committed any serious breach of trust. He knew all about her promiscuous nature, her uninhibited libidinous. That was understood and taken for granted when they had married. In that sense that was part of the contract. If she slept around, so did he. That was the arrangement and there was no question of any violation of any code of ethics or morality. Marriage for the two of them was only a matter of convenience. She needed his money and he needed her on his arm when he threw parties to impress his clients.

We had been silent for a while and he paced around the room before coming to a halt in front of me to say, 'Won't you even ask me why I killed her?'

'I couldn't care less,' I told him.

'Oh, yes, you do. I know you, you crafty old bastard. I bet you would give your arm to hear the story,' he needled me.

'Balls! I wouldn't even give my pinky,' I sneered.

He thought about it a while and then said, 'I'll tell you any way. Just to get it off my chest.'

I pretended I wasn't interested and began to move towards the bar to get another drink.

'Sit down for god's sake. I can't talk to you while you're farting around all over the countryside,' he said.

'I think a please is called for,' I said peevishly.

'Okay! Okay! Please sit down,' Menon said condescendingly.

I took my time about it by first fixing myself a drink and then strolling back to sit down.

'Remember something? You had said you won't tell me the reason why you killed her. Don't you?' I said.

'That was then and now is now,' he said dismissively. 'She had tried to kill me in Kashmir, then up at your cottage. She had even tried to get rid of me by casting spells. But all that hadn't worked. But on that day when she nearly got hit by lightning followed by the scene in her bedroom when I saw that she was no longer a woman but a man determined to sodomise me, I knew strong and pukka action was called for.'

I interrupted him, 'So, you decided to kill her. Eh?'

'You took the effing words out of my mouth, old friend. I always knew you had something in that noggin of yours. Yes. I invited her for a meeting but the meeting soon turned acrimonious. Then a veritable shouting match began and things came to a head when he got up, unzipped his fly, took out an enormous, engorged penis and began waving it in my face. That was when Swami passed his stave on to me. The one with the steel tipped end there in that corner. I think at that time I had some idea of pushing him out of the house using the stave as a prod. But Leela was too strong for that. He began to wrestle for possession and in the ensuring fracas he tripped over the carpet and fell to his knees. His face was ugly with hatred and he was spitting like an angry snake. I stood over him and the next thing I remember is that I swung the stave with all my might and cleaved his head into two. The rest you know,' he said and finished his drink.

'But you haven't told me why,' I reminded him.

'Yes. Yes the whys of it all. For one I was pissed off with the whining, the demands and the subtle threats. Then came the attempts to kill me. Then all that bullshit with the tantriks. I mean, she or rather he was becoming one hell of an ugly person. Come to think of it, I was getting to a point of buying my peace. I would have paid him off, bloody hell. But the sight of his engorged penis made me see red. Look, I may not be much of a man in bed anymore, but I am still a man. You know all over the world a man is considered disgraced if he lets himself be beaten or if he is accused of any kind of felony or doesn't pay his gambling debts. I had to establish my male credentials. I mean what kind of a man would I be if I can't scare a woman who's had a sex change operation? Tell me?' Menon said.

'I am well aware of your views on the subject of male domination,' I told him.

'What views? I know that it is the fact of life. Women are meant only for breeding and cooking. Don't give me that crap about gender equality. And please don't bore me to death with all that sanctimonious stuff about how Hindus worship the female form of Shakti. Ma Durga and all that. I am telling you that you spare the rod and you spoil the woman,' he concluded.

For a man who had gone through three marriages each more violence-ridden than the other, Menon was one stupid arsehole. I told him so. But it had no effect on him.

'Ah! I didn't commit violence against a woman, now did I? I killed a man and that is a manly thing to do, defend one's honour and all that. I bet you would have opened your arsehole and taken it in your rump,' Menon snorted.

I didn't make a retort to that because by now I had concluded that the man needed to be put in a straitjacket.

'Menon, I am going to call the doctor if you don't calm down,' I warned him.

'Calm down? Me? Why, I am the coolest guy going around. There's nothing wrong with me. See I have two hands, two legs, two eyes, one limp penis and a smooth tongue. Isn't that cool?' he sniggered.

In such a situation your choices are limited. I knew what I had to do and did it. I got up and calmly walked out of the door. Once out of the gate I broke into a sort of a trot and with some luck saw an auto cruising by. I boarded it before the driver refused to take me, which is quite common in Delhi, pulled out a hundred rupee note and told him to take me to the Interstate Bus Terminus as fast as he could. Once there I boarded the first bus heading to the hills.

Menon may have lost his senses but he was not such a fool as to believe that one day the law would not catch up with him. He had broken the law and got away with it but that was a matter of tax evasion or planning, as he called it. Murder was murder. You can call it by any name you choose – ethnic cleansing, crime of passion or whatever. My exit from the scene was in no way a very comforting thought for him. I knew too much. I knew where the body was hidden, how the murder had been committed and how the murdered person was Leela after a sex change.

Back in my cottage in the hills I sat under the plum tree, sipped my rum and water and pondered over Menon's future. I wanted to punish him and had already set the ball rolling. His business had gone downhill and how. He was busted.

The monsoon clouds rolled in from the valley in continuous waves. There was a break in the weather and the sun shone fiercely for the brief period that it showed its face. Then it was eclipsed by another black cloud and soon the mist covered everything. Droplets of water condensed on the front of my pullover, fogged my glasses and visibility was reduced to a few feet. For a moment I thought I saw Leela sailing through the mist. But the apparition was gone. I felt a cold shiver run down my back and decided it was time to go inside.

The rain came down in sheets, drumming on the tin roof till you could hardly hear yourself think. The roof gutters spilled over and water gushed out of the spouts with an understated vehemence. In the nearby storm drain a veritable roar could be heard as the rainwater whooshed down the hill carrying with it the town's dirt, discarded plastic bags, driftwood and small boulders. The jungle was silent. No bird sounds except for the irritating drip, drip of raindrops.

I sat in front of the typewriter but nothing came out. After sometime I got up and began to pace the room. In between occasional sips of my drink I tried to work out a final solution for Menon. I had the feeling that I was sitting on the roof of the world and everything was lying at my feet. I could do whatever I pleased. For the past few years I had been feeling low, disgusted with myself for being at the mercy of fellows like Menon. I was now liberated from that sense of being a bonded handmaiden to a man who I basically despised. I did not like his business ethics, his personal ethics. Come to think of it, I didn't like that man. But I persisted with him. Why? Because I was undecided, a drifter, a man given to shape his life from day to day and a believer in destiny?

The realization that I was a free man gave me ideas. Ideas of grandeur, of a feeling akin to being a super strong despot, somebody like Napoleon or a Midas. Nothing could go wrong for me now. It was a strange feeling. I was somewhere between dreaming and being awake. The state of the mind where one likes to believe that nothing is impossible. A very dangerous state of mind. How dangerous it can be was to become evident soon.

By late in the day there was a let up in the rain. I put on my gumboots, took an umbrella and decided to go for a stroll. Doggie, who had been cooped up inside the house for a larger part of the day, got up enthusiastically and ran in front of me as we set off for our walk. Raindrops sat atop blades of grass that glistened in the feeble sunlight. The birds had come out of their hiding places and were madly chirping and flitting from tree to tree in an attempt to dry their water-soaked feathers. It was a different world from the one I had run away.

But that world was never very far away. On my walk I met Doc Rawat who was rushing off to attend a call. He stopped his car and asked me when I had returned. I told him.

'And, how is your friend Menon?' he asked.

'Progressively getting worse,' I told him.

'What's that supposed to mean?'

'Well, it means what I said.'

'Your pals are all one of a kind. What about that siren Leela?' he asked.

'That is a long story, doc. You'll have to switch off the car and get out if you want to hear it,' I told him.

Curiosity got the better of the doctor who turned the ignition off and got out of the car. He lit a cigarette and said, 'So what's the news from down there?'

'Not good. Not good at all. Leela is dead,' I told him.

'Well, that was to be expected. I suppose her liver gave up on her?' he said dispassionately.

'Well, not exactly. She was murdered.'

That took the doctor aback and he wanted to know how and why.

'People get murdered. Everyone doesn't die of cancer or cirrhosis or old age. Or has the fact escaped you?'

'But why?' the doctor said.

'Why? That I can't decide on, as yet. But I can tell you that she was killed because she was becoming too much of an embarrassment to Menon.'

'An embarrassment? Did the fat bugger have her bumped off?' The doctor watched American movies with a vengeance.

'No. He killed her,' I said and felt a very heavy weight lift off my shoulders. I had told someone else the truth. My burden was now the doctor's.

'I think I'll forget what you just told me,' a visibly shocked doctor said.

Without a goodbye he got into the car and with a wave took off. That much for confessions. People, I have learnt, don't want to hear about your troubles. Such things are contagious. Never know when one can catch the bug, is the general refrain. Best to stay away. The doctor was a perfect example.

I aborted the idea of continuing my walk. I felt light headed, almost dreamy. I had told someone the terrible secret that I was carrying. The burden had been passed on. Or could it? I had only got a temporary reprieve. Maybe bought some more time. But how long was the doctor supposed to keep the secret. He had said that he had not heard me by which I suppose he meant that he was not going to talk about the murder. With these and other depressing thoughts I turned around and began the walk back home.

28

In the eventuality it was Mishti who went to the police. I pictured her in the hot, stuffy room of the police station telling some inspector about the missing Leela. The inspector taking down notes, asking her to repeat herself, until she got irritated enough to tell him off. Then the inspector asking her if she had some suspect or suspects, and she immediately and categorically mentioning Menon's name. No, 'I think', no, 'may be's'. Menon it was. The inspector, as they usually did, said he would investigate the matter and let her know.

But Mishti being Mishti wasn't the type to give up easily. She knew someone higher up in the police. She went to him and told him what she knew. The big shot policeman did what his types do. He assured her of all help and after she left promptly forgot about the matter. After all, who was he to bother about some missing woman when he had to look after the security of the nation or at least the nation's leaders.

I got to know about Mishti's goings on by a desperate phone call from Menon. He said he was sorry for his crude and rude behaviour. He begged me to forgive him. When I refused to commit myself he broke into tears and said I could have whatever I wanted. He had finally been brought to heel. Menon blamed the 'bitch' Mishti for all his troubles. The inspector had come to call on him several times and Menon said he had tried to bribe him but the man was playing hard to get. Could I please come down and handle the matter, he begged.

Grudgingly I agreed. He told me the car was on its way to pick me up and I should be ready for a long stay.

I reached Delhi fully prepared to see a broken Menon. But what surprised me was that though the man was down he was not out. He was drinking as usual but had his temper and nerves under control. This was a vindictive Menon. He was like a dangerous cobra waiting in the darkness, hissing and spitting as he waited for his prey. Or more like a predatory man-eating shark cruising some beach and waiting to snap his jaws around some hapless swimmer, preferably the unfortunate Mishti.

To me he was his most affable self. If I had not known him I would have said that the man was well composed and totally in possession of all his senses. But the fact was that the man was mad, stark raving mad. One had to look deep into his eyes to see the madness but he had covered them with dark sunglasses.

'What's with the sunglasses?' I asked him.

'Oh! That? Nothing. I have a touch of old Jai Bangla. You know?' he said.

Conjunctivitis or old Jai Bangla was a passable explanation for a man wearing dark glasses inside his house. I noticed Swami wasn't in attendance. As if reading my thoughts Menon said, 'Help yourself to a drink. Swami has gone to his village. I have to make do without him.'

That was surprising because Swami in all the years I had known Menon had never taken any leave. I often wondered if the man had a home except Menon's. For all practical purposes the man was on the lam after he had murdered his cousin in a violent fit of jealousy. Going home would mean hanging himself because the police would arrest him for sure.

'I was under the impression that the man didn't have a home. I mean he had run away, hadn't he?' I said.

'Yes, but that was a long time ago,' Menon said.

That didn't go down well with me. I gave a couldn't-care-less shrug and said, 'So what's new?'

'Ah! That's something we have to talk about. Look why don't you freshen up. Have a shower and all. We'll go out to dinner to one of these fancy joints and I'll bring you up to scratch,' Menon said.

I could see nothing wrong with that and with a see-you-later disappeared to my usual room on the first floor.

❧❧

Dinner was a bit of a liquid affair. We went through a bottle of wine along with several Scotches and by the time the brandy was called for I was truly sozzled. Menon seemed to be untroubled and had tucked into his dinner with his usual gusto. After the plates had been cleared Menon launched his spiel.

He began by saying that the 'bitch' Mishti had instigated a police investigation and he had already been visited several times by one Inspector Shiv Ram.

'What have you told him?' I mumbled.

'I haven't told him anything. I told him I hadn't seen Leela since I was last in your place and had no idea where she was. But the man isn't satisfied. He's been to the house three times already. On his last visit I offered him some money but he refused. Ever heard of an honest cop?'

'Maybe, then maybe not,' I managed to croak.

'Look. This Shiv Ram is obviously on the take. He's fishing around because he doesn't have any solid proof. And no way is he going to get it. The only witness is Swami and I've packed him off to the Dubai office. So, he's out of the country and won't be coming back in a hurry,' Menon said.

'I thought you said Swami had gone home,' I said.

'Same thing,' Menon said.

I was drunk but not that drunk to not know the difference between going home and buggering off to Dubai. But Menon was like that. He could make anything look very easy or very complicated. Like making Swami disappear at will. I must have been dropping off because I felt Menon lifting me by my elbow and guiding me out of the restaurant. I suppose we made it to his car because I don't remember anything after that except waking up in my bed with a terrible hangover.

There are all kinds of benefits of hangovers. The usual symptoms of a damning headache, nausea and loss of memory are replaced with introspection, resolves to never touch a drop again and so on and so forth. But the best one is the luxury of lying around in bed feeling like death warmed over. And so it was in Menon's house the morning after my arrival in Delhi. There was no rich smell of imported coffee wafting up from the kitchen and the realization that Swami wasn't around hit me hard. I crawled out of bed, moaning and groaning and sleepwalked downstairs.

I found Menon pottering around in the kitchen and with a cheerful good morning he announced that coffee would be ready in no time. That was in itself surprising. Menon was one grouch early in the morning. The coffee came as promised and I gratefully gulped the beverage.

'So, what's the agenda for today?' Menon asked.

I looked at him and as he slowly came into focus I noticed that he wasn't dressed and seemed in no hurry to go anywhere. He looked at ease and hadn't bothered to look at the newspapers either. The man was not behaving as he normally did. This in itself was alarming enough. He did not have the preoccupied air about him that marked him as a high-powered executive. Lolling around that morning he looked like some kind of a retired university professor who had plenty of time on his hands and nothing more important to do than to pick up the household groceries.

'Don't you have to go to work?' I asked him.

'Work? That's history, old pal. I've closed down the shop and all that. I've got a whole lot of other things to do than to worry about a silly business,' he told me.

'What other things? Don't tell me you are thinking of taking up painting or writing or something equally frivolous,' I said.

'Nothing like that. But let's get you organized for the day.'

And so we got organized. What this meant was that I was to approach the Inspector Shiv Ram and see if I could convince him to lay off. Menon said he had something else to do and disappeared. With nothing better to do I took the car and went to the police station.

Delhi police stations are in a class by themselves. They don't have the impressive structures that such posts have in Bombay, Calcutta or Madras. In Old Delhi or the walled city the thanas are in keeping with their cousins in the older cities. In New Delhi, they are as new as the city and its denizens. In other words the police stations reflect the mindsets of the people who live in that area. In the affluent Defence Colony the police station has a certain air of affluence about it. But that is misleading.

I asked for Inspector Shiv Ram from a clerk sitting behind an impressive pile of paper work. He brusquely told me that he wouldn't be in for another hour or so. I could wait and he pointed to a bench in one corner. It was still early for the police station. Some petty cases were being taken to the courts. They were the types who had been detained overnight for being drunk, a motley group of whores ugly and garish in the morning light, a pickpocket or a petty thief and a rather distinguished looking white haired gentleman who I vaguely recognized as having been a senior diplomat. I wondered what he was in for as this was the last place one expected to run into a man of his status. He had a blank look like a sleepwalker and he was gently escorted to a police jeep.

Curious and with nothing better to do I had followed him outside and as he got into the jeep I waved to him. He didn't respond. As the jeep pulled away a Mercedes drove in and a young man got out and walked inside. He greeted the clerk sitting behind the pile of files as if he was a long lost friend.

'Where's the old man?' he asked him.

'Oh, he just left. You can catch him at the Patiala House Courts,' the clerk told him.

The young man took out a packet of cigarettes, offered one to the clerk who took it but put it in his shirt pocket. They smiled conspiratorially and the young man took a long drag, blew a plume of smoke in the air and said, 'We'll meet at the usual place.'

He left and I bcgan to walk towards the bench when I heard the clerk tell to one and all assembled, 'See! What the world has come to. This is kalyug when a son comes in to have his father arrested. He should have brought a good nazrana for the SHO to have his father released. No. All he does is brings in money to have his father produced in court.'

He made sounds of disapproval but that didn't stop him from getting up and going outside where he met the young man 'at the same place'. He could be seen smoking and talking and after a while he came in and told me that Shiv Ram was waiting for me in the canteen. For that piece of information I was supposed to pay him and I grudgingly slipped him a fifty-rupee note.

The canteen was inside a tin shed. A row of benches and tables was all the furniture. Shiv Ram sat in a corner sipping tea. I recognized him by Menon's description.

'So, Menon sahab has sent you,' he said after I told him why I had come.

Shiv Ram was a tall and good-looking man. From his accent he sounded like a Jat, notorious for their crudity. But that was misleading. Crude he might have been but he was one shrewd guy. He wasn't wearing a uniform and in plainclothes he looked like any of the hundreds of real estate agents that had mushroomed on the periphery of Delhi.

But Shiv Ram had obviously no such ambition. He was making his money comfortably by milking the ones who were milking the others. He made that very clear right from the start when he began the meeting with, 'So, Menon sahab has sent you.'

I must have looked the anti-thesis of what he was used to

seeing. Here I was longhaired, bearded, obviously a bookish type with little or no exposure to the cuts and thrusts of city life. A bit on the moral crusader side, the types who are not welcome in police stations all over the country.

His gaze travelled all over me from head to foot like he was viewing a piece of sculpture. Then he lazily waved me down to sit on the bench across him. A tea was ordered and it came in a chipped cup and a pool of its residue in the saucer. I threw the pool into the mud below the table and took a sip of what was a very sugary concoction. That wasn't very encouraging either and so I pushed the cup and saucer to one side and began to get ready for the negotiations.

'You don't like,' Shiv Ram said and pointed to the rejected cup and saucer.

I grimaced and shrugged my shoulders.

'Perhaps, it is beer time,' Shiv Ram said.

I shrugged again.

Shiv Ram snapped his fingers and a cold beer appeared which rather surprised me. After all this was a police station or maybe the canteen didn't strictly belong in the area that made up the police station. Apparently it didn't because Shiv Ram encouraged me to go ahead.

'What about you?' I asked.

'Me? I don't drink,' the inspector said.

Caught between the devil and the deep sea, as it were, I sipped my beer and put in a tentative question: 'Why are you asking Menon all these questions about his wife. You know she left him some years ago. They are divorced and she lives on her own. He has no contact with her. So, he can't be of much help.'

Shiv Ram just looked at me, his beady eyes signaling that he was nobody's fool. This was my first brush with the police in a big city. Back in the mountains the police were a friendly lot and besides there was little that one could do there that could be kept a secret. On top of that crime of any sort was unheard of unless you call running away with someone's wife or daughter a felony. It was almost as if the man was reading my mind because his eyes seemed to be saying, *But in the big city things are different*.

'Where are you from?' he asked as if I was some kind of an alien.

'You haven't answered my question,' I told him.

'Oh! But you haven't asked me one,' he retorted.

This was going to be one of those conversations where two people keep asking questions and no one replies. It was like talking at cross-purposes.

'I said why are you bothering Menon sahab about his wife?' in a voice one uses to address a child or a nitwit.

'But I am not,' Shiv Ram said in the same tone.

'Well, it looks like you don't want to answer me. Or at any rate you don't know the answer. So when you can come up with one do let me know,' I said and began to walk away.

'Wait. Just a minute,' the inspector said.

So, I waited while he ambled up to me and said, 'Look, you seem like an educated man. Myself B.A. Honours, Delhi University. But you don't know how we work. We, meaning the police. Now if you had come with an offer of your son for my daughter I would have been down on my knees doing your bidding. The problem is you've come to ask for my son. You see.'

Well, I didn't see and told him so.

'You will, you will. Meet me at the Japanese restaurant in the market. I like Japanese food. 8 p.m. sharp,' he said and walked away towards the station. I looked at his retreating back and wondered what to make of what he had said.

Inspector Shiv Ram was sitting on his motorcycle outside the Japanese restaurant when I walked up to him later that evening.

'Should we go inside?' I suggested.

'No. No. I want to take you somewhere else,' he said, started his motorcycle and motioned to me to ride pillion. He deftly wheeled the bike through the traffic and soon we were on the main road heading towards Nizamuddin. I had kept quiet because I wanted to see where he was going to take me. As things stood I didn't know better and I felt it was wiser to let things develop the way he wanted it.

And develop they did. We stopped outside a restaurant in the rather seedy market and walked in. It was quite nice, air-conditioned with a tastefully done décor. In one corner sitting alone was Mishti.

For a moment my heart missed a beat. This was the last place I would have expected to meet up with that corpulent woman.

'Hello Mishti,' I said for want of anything else.

She gave me a frosty smile and signaled me to take a seat. There was a crafty look in her mean eyes that seemed to be saying that she had me where she wanted me. And that also by my short and curly. The inspector came and sat down next to me. They obviously knew each other and under the table I felt Mishti press her knee against the inspector's. They were a chummy lot, I told myself.

'So, that bastard Menon wants you to talk to Shiv Ram,' Mishti began.

I nodded observing all the time how she was addressing the inspector rather familiarly. The two were already on intimate terms and it was easy to see that the inspector was doing to her what I wasn't. The other thing that was very obvious was that Mishti knew something I didn't.

'To begin with you can tell him that there is nothing to talk about with Shiv Ram. Now you have to talk to me. If that bastard wants to stay away from thc gallows and save his ugly hide tell him to begin coughing up money. To begin with, I want five lakh down as a gesture of goodwill. When you have delivered the money, I will then tell you more. See you,' she said and coolly walked away. Shiv Ram grinned and winked lasciviously.

I was paralysed, so to say. To begin with her presence there, then her knowledge about what was going on and her being chummy and all with the inspector had put me at a disadvantage. I felt a numbness descend on me and my hands and feet felt cold and lifeless. This was something that was totally unplanned and not bargained for. What to do? a wise man once said.

Caught in what seemed to be a storm that was building up and threatening to wipe everything from its path I had no option but to tell Shiv Ram that I had to consult Menon before I could commit to anything. Obviously, this was blackmail but the questions that kept coming back to my mind were how did Mishti know and how much. Or was she simply calling a bluff?

The inspector saw the perplexed look on my face and said, 'Take your time about it and while you are at it make sure my cut is also included.'

He offered me a drink which I declined so horrified I was with the monstrosity of the whole thing. Blackmail is one of those things that like a leech sucks you dry. Once you give in, the demands never stop. On the other hand they intensify till such time as you drop dead. Or do something equally nasty.

❧❧

Menon was naturally livid when I told him about Mishti's demand. He called her names, raved and ranted and all but set fire to the house. I sat in a corner nursing a drink and waiting for some kind of a solution to come to mind.

'The bitch knows? The question is what and how much,' Menon echoed my thoughts.

'I suppose the inspector has been briefing her. I can't see how she can even guess at the truth of the matter. Your ex-wife has disappeared and no one but no one knows how and where. There is no way that I or Swami will spill the beans. So that leaves you. Did you say anything to the inspector that might have aroused his suspicions?' I asked.

'Do you take me for a fool?' Menon shouted. 'Why should I tell that bastard of an inspector anything?'

Yes, why should he. It would be suicidal. Menon was capable of murder but suicide was out of the question. He valued his thick skin too much to do anything remotely connected to cause him hurt. His well-being came first and last. The rest of the people around him could be dying as far as he was concerned. Men like Menon don't get there where he had by being altruistic, forgiving and compassionate. He was a downright bastard if there ever was one and god knows how much I wanted him to hang at the end of a rope for killing Leela. But I was in it too and had to think ways of saving my skin first.

It was getting to be quite late and I didn't think we would be able to address the problem properly till the morning. I went off to my room and had a restless night. Menon didn't sleep a wink but kept pacing the drawing room till dawn broke and the chatter of birds on his lawn woke him from whichever world he was inhabiting at the moment.

Menon must have thought deeply about what to do with Mishti. I say must have because when I came down the next morning he was up and about and said he was going to do something about that bitch which meant Mishti, of course. I asked him what his plan of action was and he said something like wait and see before storming out of the house. He had retained his Mercedes but had dismissed the driver and drove himself. Menon was a maniac behind the wheel and perfectly suited for Delhi's traffic.

I made coffee, read the morning papers, had a shower and did the usual morning things that most sane people do. Since there was no Swami around I made myself an omelette that I downed for breakfast. I was at a loose end and with nothing better to do went over to the police station to find Shiv Ram and chat with him. Going to police stations can be addictive I was finding out. What egged on my curiosity was the way Shiv Ram went about the business of implementing law and order.

It intrigued me to learn that as the investigating officer in the missing Leela case he hardly spent an hour a day chasing down a lead since there were no leads. He had done the usual police work of putting in an ad in the papers, asked the husband, the neighbours, known friends of Leela and had struck gold with Mishti who took no time in having an ally like him between her legs. From what Shiv Ram told me it was Mishti's idea to milk Menon for all that he was worth because as Mishti put it the 'bastard knew something'.

Call it a woman's instinct or plain lucky guesswork, Mishti was on the right track. And Menon had seen that. That morning he had gone to her house to re-negotiate the blackmail amount and as he told me later the 'bitch wasn't moving her fat arse on her demand'. I tried to reason with Shiv Ram as we drank a cup of over sweetened tea in the canteen at the police station but he too wouldn't budge. I hinted that I could go to someone higher up and all the man said was that I was welcome to do that because in the end everything would come back to him as he had to prepare the final action taken report.

In a way it was a wasted morning and so I returned to the house to wait for Menon. He arrived shortly afterwards with the 'bitch won't move her fat arse' report. I told him that we could pay the two off and get them off our backs but Menon flatly turned down the suggestion on the grounds that they would keep asking for more. Here he was right. Blackmailers do that all the time and at any rate paying up is in a way an admission of guilt of one sort or the other.

Menon said we could go out for lunch to his club and I agreed because that was better than doing nothing.

A good lunch can sometimes throw up some good ideas. Like Napoleon one has to believe that an army marches on it's stomach. Menon sure did because he came up with the startling proposition that both Mishti and her lover could be done away with half the money they had asked for and nobody would be wiser. He said he knew someone who knew someone who would take a 'supari' or a contract kill.

I knew about these contract kills from newspapers and while they were quite the rage in Bombay one didn't hear of them in Delhi. But I didn't like the idea.

Menon saw my displeasure and knew he had spoiled my lunch for me. Perhaps, that was the effect he wanted. When I told him that I was washing my hands of the whole project he simply smiled and said, 'As you wish.' That was tame coming from him till it suddenly struck me that I too could be on his hit list. He was devious, Menon was. I told him so. He vehemently denied it saying that he wouldn't ever think of offing me when he knew he could buy my silence. And to settle the matter, as it were, he whipped out his cheque book and made me a cheque of ten lakh which was enough for me to survive for another ten years.

I manfully waved the cheque away and told him to keep it for his contract killers. Actually I was tempted to take it and stash it in my pocket and make a beeline for the nearest bank and cash it. But I didn't do that. You see there was nothing to stop Menon from both paying me and then bumping me off. He was that kind of a man. And as I watched him from day to day he was getting the maniac look more often that he masked with a big smile.

I pushed back my chair and rose to leave. Menon said he would drop me wherever I wanted to go but I told him I wasn't going anywhere and would prefer to walk and get my thoughts in order. I told him I would catch up with him at his house.

It is a short walk from Menon's club to Defence Colony and as I plodded along in my loping hill-man style I pondered the pros and cons of hanging on with Menon.

The problem simply boiled down, as far as I could see, to the fact that I was a key witness now that Swami had disappeared or been made to disappear. I had no way of knowing whether the fat swine was alive or dead. For all I knew he was fish food somewhere in the Arabian Sea. And as I walked along I had a distinct feeling of being observed. I looked over my shoulder a couple of times but saw nothing and shrugged off the thought to a case of the nerves.

However, things changed rather suddenly. As I turned into the lane leading to Menon's house a car came and braked in front of me. The rear window slid down and a man with Leela's eyes looked at me, smiled and opened the door to invite me in. For a moment I stared back and then my knees buckled, bells sounded in my ears and I think I fainted.

When I came to I was lying on a soft bed in a neatly furnished room. Across from me sitting in a chair and smoking was a dapper looking man in a dark pinstripe suit, longish hair neatly parted in the middle and brushed back. He smiled at me and it was Leela's smile right down to the dimple on his right cheek and the twisted upper lip which men had found so attractive. For a moment I thought I was looking at a man who had an uncanny resemblance to the late and departed Leela. And in that instance I remembered that Leela was no longer Leela but a man.

I raised myself groggily on one elbow and stared at the man who was a spitting image of Leela. As my eyes came into sharper focus I noticed Mishti sitting in a chair on the other side of the bed and smiling down at me. Both of them had drinks in their hands and it was Leela who spoke first.

'Hi! Remember me?' he said. The voice husky as ever.

I cleared my throat to say something but no words came out.

Leela then stretched out and kissed me on the cheek which I found both repulsive and strangely attractive. A man was kissing me, as far as I could understand, and that man looked like Leela. I wasn't in the men-kissing league, as yet. That sort of shook me out of my dumb mode and I said, 'Who are you?'

'Leela, your old friend Leela, dummy,' the man said.

I looked at Mishti for confirmation and she smiled and nodded. I sat up in bed and got a grip on myself. Shaking my head like a wet dog I glared at Leela. 'What the hell?' I was able to mutter. Leela didn't have to change her name. There were both female and male Leelas.

Some sense of normal was returning to my legs and I swung them off the bed and managed to stand up. I was still dressed in the same clothes I had put on to go for lunch with Menon and as I slowly began to gather my senses I realized I was in the presence of Leela the man. My brain told me that he was buried in Menon's drawing room and my eyes told me he was alive and sitting right in front of me.

'What the hell?' I said once again like a stuck record.

'That's a strange way to greet a long lost friend,' Leela said.

'Long lost? But I thought you were dead and buried,' I told Leela.

'I was and I wasn't,' Leela said enigmatically.

By now I was more or less normal. Mishti had pushed a drink into my hand and after a long sip I asked, 'What's that supposed to mean?'

'Go and wash your face and I'll tell you. It is a long story,' Leela said.

I did as ordered and as I dried myself in the bathroom and looked at the bottles of aftershave, shaving brush and cream and other things neatly laid out, I realized I was in Leela's flat. The one I had visited with Mishti not so long ago. Then it was as if the place had not been in use for sometime and now it looked spic and span. I used the w.c., pulled the chain and looking fairly presentable returned to the room, which as I looked around I noticed was Leela's bedroom.

Leela and Mishti had moved to the front drawing room and I joined them there, rather confused and for the moment lost for words. Leela in her new avtar, sex change et al, looked quite elegant and I said so. He smiled and said that it was a miracle of modern surgery. Mishti said he was 'soo handsome' in such a gushing way that for a moment I thought she had forgotten that Leela used to be a woman till only a few months back.

As usual Leela took the initiative and said, 'Take a pew and listen to a good yarn, if you still care for other people's stories.'

I did as I was told and duly armed with a fresh drink leaned back in my chair to hear what Leela had to say. It was quite a mouthful, interestingly unbelievable yet without any doubt the truth and only the whole truth. When one heard it for the first time it didn't make much sense but as the contents sank deeper into the brain the whole story made complete sense.

32

Leela began his story after his return from my cottage in the hills. He said he had lost all hope of ever getting more money out of Menon. His tantriks had failed miserably, their black magic turning out to be overwhelmed by Menon's brand of the same stuff. In his new persona he had discarded his feminine attributes, begun to think like a man, dress, walk and talk like one. It was then that Leela had come up with the idea of suborning Swami.

Like most men with his kind of past Swami was vulnerable. When Leela and Menon were still enjoying domestic bliss, Leela had come across a letter for Swami from Kerala. It was a postcard and out of sheer boredom and curiosity she had managed to read, in her halting Malayali, parts of it. From that she had garnered that Swami had a past that had made him stay away from his home all these years. In effect the letter mentioned the murder of Swami's cousin and how after all these years it had been more or less forgotten. The letter advised Swami to come home now that there was no chance of the police taking any action against him. She didn't know who the sender was but what she knew was that she had Swami by his balls. That information long held by Leela was now put to good use when she confronted Swami one afternoon when Menon was away on one of his trips.

When Swami came to know what Leela knew he was mortified. He was no longer the young brave man but a frightened and aging man who knew of no one except Menon who would give him shelter. On top of it Leela was no longer a woman and he knew that though he could physically overpower him he could not beat him in the mental department. He was easily in a pliable state and Leela then came up with the idea that he was quick to grab because it gave him a chance to run to some place where Menon could never get him and neither the police. The only reason he continued to work for Menon was simply because Menon knew of his past and could use it against him any time he felt like it. In his heart of hearts Swami despised Menon but circumstances were such that he had to continue behaving like a faithful dog. It had hurt his self-esteem for such a long time that he had almost forgotten he even had one.

According to Leela, he had one day gone to Menon's house and after making sure that Menon was drunk enough teased and goaded him to strike him. His ultimate threat to bugger the bastard had Menon see red and he had grabbed Swami's stave and hit Leela on the forehead. It was a feeble and glancing blow and Leela could have easily dodged it. But instead he didn't and with a great show of pain had collapsed to the ground. Swami who was watching all this from his vantage position in the kitchen had then come running in, grabbed the stave from Menon and pretended to deliver the coup de grace. Menon had blacked out because of the drink and the exertion and Swami had taken him to his room.

Then later in the night Leela and Swami had broken the original marble slab, dug a portion of the floor and made a mock grave. Leela had then disappeared to parts unknown. In the morning Menon had woken up with a faint memory of some kind of violence and when he asked Swami about it he learnt that Leela had been killed and buried right there in his drawing room. He ordered Swami to get a new marble slab and cover the grave and obliterate all traces of Leela's presence in the house on that fateful night.

Menon then went in for some heavy drinking and once when he was slightly less sozzled Swami suggested he summon the writer from the hill station to take the plot forward. Of course, the scenario had been crafted by Leela himself. He had quite accurately guessed that I would be revolted by the horror of the whole thing and do something to bring about the downfall of Menon. As events unfolded I came down from the mountain and did my bit by frightening Menon and ruining his business with some help from Mishti and her so called collection of tapes and recordings of Leela's voice. These had all been set up by Leela.

I was now acutely aware of the intricate and almost Byzantine working of Leela's mind. Sitting in that drawing room and listening to the two of them chortling with glee over their success I was quite miffed. I also felt used and soiled. Before this revelation I had been riding a morally righteous high, doing the right thing by Leela and all that. But now I was having second thoughts.

From all appearances Leela was getting the most out of the whole venture while I was just a simple cog. In that sense Leela was no different from Menon. He had used me when it suited him and even now Leela and Mishti were making me the conduit to milk Menon of his money. The more I thought about it the more I felt like a village oaf sucked into the sophistry of these clever people. Well, I reasoned, if that was the way it was going to be why don't I cut myself into the deal for 'services rendered'. I could also be as greedy as the rest of them.

While all these and other ideas were roaring around in my head Leela was watching me and possibly reading my thoughts. As he fetched me another drink he said, 'You know you are a nice guy. I mean standing up for me and all that. But you are a bit too naïve. Take my advice and you will be all right. I mean to give you a part of the loot you get out of that bastard. Let's call it collector's fee, shall we?'

Put like that, it didn't sound too awful. After all I was spending sweat and time on it and deserved to get something for my efforts, dishonest as the whole thing was.

I seemed to remember I had a conscience somewhere but it was a fading memory and as the figures began to roll around the walls of the drawing room I too began to dance to their tune. It was a sweet kind of music that had me dreaming of lazy days on the beaches of Goa and the Med, soaking in the sun and rum and ogling the bikini clad beauties.

33

The plan to sting Menon was on. I was told to go to him and ask him for the five lakh that Mishti wanted and another five lakh to keep the inspector quiet. I did as told and conveyed the news to Menon when I returned to his house. As usual he asked me where I had been and I told him that after leaving him at the club I had met Shiv Ram and he had repeated the demand. I also told him that time was of the essence and the faster we paid up the faster we could get out of their clutches.

But Menon was not having any of that. He wanted to stick to his original plan and told me so. I shrugged and said it was his life and he could do what he liked with it but I was getting out. Menon pleaded with me to hang on till he got Mishti and that inspector bumped off. Then I could go to Timbucktoo as far as he was concerned, he told me.

It was important to stick around with Menon to know what his plans were so that I could accordingly inform my new-found allies. Menon had no idea of what he was in for. He arranged for the hitman to come in from Bombay and on the day the hit was planned I told the inspector who promptly picked up the man from a Paharganj hotel, near the New Delhi railway station.

Police interrogation is a polite word for the third degree. Shiv Ram told me he put chilly up the arse of the hit man and he spilled the beans naming all those involved. Menon was going to be the paymaster and that was that. Armed with that knowledge Shiv Ram landed up at Menon's door.

This was another grand occasion for blackmail but the stakes were up a thousand-fold. Shiv Ram told Menon that he had an open and shut case against him and that the contract killer had 'confessed' and was willing to do so in front of a magistrate which would mean the high jump for Menon.

This time around Menon knew he had no choice and if he was to get out of the trap he had to cough up. Shiv Ram began his demand with a crore each for Mishti and him. Menon pleaded for a discount, which was promptly turned down and now with his back to the wall Menon coughed up the money, which was delivered to Leela.

I had kept away from the house deliberately and it was quite late by the time I returned. Menon asked me where I had been and I told him I had gone to see some friends and besides it was none of his business. That night Menon began to drink again. He was in a bellicose mood vowing by all the gods that he would get Mishti and Shiv Ram one of these days. I watched him from a safe distance as he planned his next move. It was obvious he was short on cash and now the Bombay people were baying for his blood because they felt that he had betrayed them to the police. He already had a hit man on his tail and it was simply a question of time before he got him.

This hit man was an interesting type. He had been to the house already and in the meeting at which I was present had asked Menon to pay him double his fees as one of their kind had been betrayed to the police. Menon said he needed time to think and the hit man said he only had twenty-four hours as he was a busy man and had to get back to Bombay. The money or your life, the man had said before leaving.

Knowing he was caught between the devil and the deep sea he decided to give in. The hit man would shoot him on sight. The police might take their time but the end result would be the same. There was a slight chance of something going wrong with the police investigation and he could get away, but there was little chance of the hitman missing him or anything as simple as that. So, he paid. Another considerable amount. It was as if his fortune was melting away in front of his eyes.

I should have felt sorry to see him being drained like that. But I didn't. I went and told Leela the whole story about the second hit man. He laughed some more and said the bastard was getting his just desserts. For these nuggets of information Leela was paying me handsomely and I was laughing all the way to the bank. It was the easiest money I had earned and there was no way Menon was going to know about it. In a manner of speaking taking his money indirectly instead of from him made me feel like I had accomplished something. Here I was not simply at his beck and call, a demeaning business to put it mildly. I was earning the money or so I told myself.

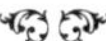

Autumn was round the corner in Delhi and there was a nip in the air. I was riding high on my ill-gotten wealth. Leela was good company and I no longer felt threatened by his sexuality. He laughed and joked a lot that made up for the feeling of gloom I felt whenever Mishti was around. She was no longer hitting at me now that she had the inspector doing his bit. Menon was getting back to his old drinking ways and was often very maudlin. He had dumped his mistress and was usually found lolling around in the house. The place itself began to wear a seedy look now that Swami wasn't around. Dust covered most things in the house and Menon couldn't have cared less. The bathrooms were dirty as no cleaning woman dared to come to the house. Menon was often heard shouting at no one and talking to himself. The word in the servant community was that Menon had gone mad.

In many ways that was true. He no longer cared about how he dressed, what he ate and his fat frame had begun to shrink as he lost weight. No one called on him and he didn't go anywhere. He was a prisoner in his own house. Rarely did he bother to get out of the Thai silk dressing gown and lungi and showers were something of the past. One day he told me to sell his crystal for whatever I could get. It was then that I realized that the man was steadily going bankrupt. I wondered what happened to his reputed fortune. After all, between Leela and the hit men he had lost only a few crores.

The story of his fortune was as convoluted as the man himself. In the last few months as bad fortune struck him on all sides he turned to his disowned son.

In what was a move to appease him for all the insults hurled at him through his growing years and his exile in London he gave him a power of attorney to control his overseas bank accounts. That would have been all right but for the fact that the acorn had not fallen very far from the oak. The son was a bigger crook than his father and the windfall that came his way had made him greedy, like the rest of us. He didn't waste time in being the prodigal son, the repentant wastrel, but began to eat of the fatted calf even before his father knew about it. In that he was aided and abated by his mother Leela who had been in touch with him over the years. Leela had, however, not told his son about his sex change.

All it took was one call from London to tell him that he no longer had any money in his Swiss and other accounts. They had been cleaned up by the son who was making up for his days of hardship. He could be seen at nightclubs, casinos and all the resorts that offered him some pleasure grandly splurging off his father's ill-gotten gains. That was the proverbial last straw and to keep himself in liquor he had begun to get rid of his crystal, dinner sets and other household items.

I was a mute witness to his destruction and while I could have left him and moved back to my mountain refuge I waited till the last. Menon still had his Mercedes but the time was coming when that too would be up for sale. Since there were no meals being cooked in the house I more often than not ate with Leela in some restaurant or the other. Sometimes we would be joined by our partners in crime, Mishti and Shiv Ram. No one seemed to feel any remorse for Menon's ill-fortune, and why would they. They had been his victims one way or the other and they gloated over the fact that they had screwed the black bastard.

The Mercedes disappeared one day and Menon flush with funds suggested we go and celebrate. My heart wasn't in it but I tagged along anyway to his favourite watering hole. That was a bit of a torture as he shamelessly threw money around. He abused the waiters and the next moment appeased them with huge tips. I was getting disgusted and after a while I rose and walked away. He didn't even notice my departure.

He didn't come home that night and for the next few nights. He had checked into a hotel and was drinking all he could till he passed out. Then he would wake up again and begin the ritual. The manager called me one day and asked me to take him home as he was becoming a nuisance and hotel guests were complaining. I decided to do the old bastard one last favour. I went to the hotel and persuaded him to come home. It took a lot of persuasion and cajoling before he agreed.

After seeing nearly all the household items disappear, I noticed that a disreputable looking young man would often visit Menon. One day I asked him who he was and what was his business with the old man. He smiled ingratiatingly and told me he was a real estate agent and Menon sahab had asked him to find a buyer for his house. While going about his business he was also bringing in bottles of Indian whisky which was a far cry from the days when Menon drank only premium Scotch.

I had then tried to reason with the man but he just waved me away like a pesky fly and after several aborted attempts I gave up and let him slide into his whisky sodden world. The only thing he had kept was his giant television because he would sit in front of it the whole day long, drinking whisky, then passing out and then waking up and drinking some more in a ritual that never seemed to end.

When I told Leela that Menon was down to his bottom rupee he laughed some more and said that it was time to sink in the final hook. He asked me to keep him posted on news of the sale and he would think up of something.

One fine day when it was pleasant enough to sit in the lawn and enjoy the winter sun a fat man and his wife came and asked for Menon. They were accompanied by the broker fellah and I didn't bother to reply. Instead I gestured with my thumb indicating they could go in. The broker had as usual brought Menon's quota of whisky and I knew that a deal was about to be struck.

A deal was indeed struck and money changed hands with promises for settlement of the final amount in two weeks.

It was indeed a lot of money because the house was worth upwards of two crore and when I walked in I saw Menon sitting there in front of the television with bundles of notes spread out before him like playing cards.

'Better not leave that loot lying around,' I advised him.

'Fat all you care,' he retorted.

I shrugged, as it was pointless talking to him anymore. I had by then decided to leave his house and move in with another friend. I picked up my battered suitcase and put the few clothes I had into it and left the house without even a civilized good-bye.

Leela was informed about the sale later that day and he lost no time in sending Shiv Ram across to Defence Colony and take whatever loot he could get out of Menon. He must have got a substantial amount because Leela came over and handed me my share. It was indeed a lot of money and I began to wonder how Menon would keep himself in whisky if he was going to keep paying Leela and party.

After spending a few days in Delhi and now loaded with money I decided to head for the hills. My novel was finished and I had submitted it to a publisher in the fond hope of seeing it in print. It was time to begin work on another one and winter was the ideal time because nobody disturbed me and my lifestyle and I could write as long as I pleased. I had washed my hands of the entire Menon episode and in a manner of speaking I was rather pleased with myself at the way things had gone.

Life at my cottage began to gather its normal momentum with work and long walks with Doggie. The usual rum and pani. A bit of television and lots of sleep. From time to time my old friend the Doc would drop in and we would chat about this and that. For Christmas that year another couple came by on a short visit. They had decided to split and wanted me to be the arbitrator. I listened to their individual versions and decided they were both too far gone to live together amicably.

It was the same old bitching about this and that, money being the driving force. The children were grown up and couldn't have cared less but their fees and expenses had to be taken care of till they found suitable employment. The big question was who would they stay with. Mama or Papa?

While these and other questions were being resolved the two quarreled bitterly all the time and that Christmas weekend was only memorable because of their shouting matches.

It is amazing the kind of dirt that some married couples carry with them all their lives. Their hates, their loves, their little secrets are additional baggage they just can't wait to jettison. But the timing is what they can't find. When they reach the end of their tether they explode in a frenzy of accusations and counter accusations. Hearing them an uninterested bystander is slowly dragged into the private lives of these people. Wise words of advice are generally ignored by the warring parties as they go on relentlessly berating each other for imagined and not so imagined crimes. This washing of dirty linen makes for messy divorces and only lawyers seem to make a killing out of the whole process.

I had warned this couple of the dangers of going to court. Instead I suggested a civilized arrangement by which things could be settled amicably. But that was not to be because they haggled about everything from the kitchen silver to the dog. They left in a bad mood much to my relief though the holiday atmosphere had been marred by their hate-filled energy. It was time I took off for some change and rang up Leela to ask if it was all right for me to come down for the New Year. Leela was overjoyed to hear from me and said I could come down and stay with him as he had bought a big flat in Defence Colony and quite close to where Menon had once lived.

I took up Leela's invitation and soon found myself at his door. Leela had bought a nice house on the first floor of a bungalow with a separate entrance. We exchanged pleasantries till I asked him about Menon. He laughed and said that Menon had done the damndest thing imaginable. He had taken up abode near the tomb of Chisti Nizamuddin, become a sort of Sufi and could be seen on any day criss-crossing the road unmindful of the traffic.

This was something I had to see. Later that evening I went to Nizamuddin. After wandering around for a while I parked myself at a vantage point from where I could see people coming and going to the tomb. A little while later a dark, tallish man with unkempt hair and beard, dressed in a black kaftan came tearing out from the direction of the tomb and began criss-crossing the road. In one hand he held a cane broom, which he kept swishing around like a sword as he crossed the road. He didn't wait for the traffic to stop and as cars and trucks roared past him I feared for his life. But nothing happened and he kept doing that for a while till he, tired of it returned to his corner near the tomb where he sat down with some other ascetic looking men like him.

I strolled up to him and called softly, 'Menon.'

There was no reaction. His eyes had the blank look of an insane man or a man high on hashish. In front of him was a tin can where he apparently collected alms. It was pathetically empty. I took a hundred rupee note from my pocket and put it in the can. There was no movement or attempt to take the money. Instead, all he said was 'Come, Come . . . ' and the rest was lost in the din of the passing traffic.

Lost like his useless and contemptible life. I turned away and as I was leaving I asked another dervish hanging around if he knew who the man in the black kaftan was. He looked at him and said, 'He's just the man who crosses the road.'

There was nothing more to be said and with a self-satisfied and morally upright stand I told myself, *serves the bastard right.*

SUDHIR THAPLIYAL

An IIM graduate from Calcutta, **Sudhir Thapliyal** joined the *Statesman*, Calcutta, in 1967 and is today a freelance journalist, writer and documentary filmmaker. He has worked as a radio and TV commentator in India and abroad. He was nominated for the Rhodes Scholarship in 1967, and is also a 1972 Fellow of the World Press Institute, St Paul, Minn (USA).

Author of *Hello! Mister Tee* and *War at Lambidhar*, many of his short stories and features have been published in leading Indian magazines and Sunday supplements, including the *Statesman Literary Supplement* and the *Financial Times*, London. He has written the screenplay of a telefilm based on Ruskin Bond's novel *Room on the Roof*. Currently he is working on a screenplay for a Bollywood producer.

An avid trekker, mountaineer and naturalist he has been nearly everywhere in the Indian Himalayas. He has travelled widely in the United States, Europe and India. He was a member of Edmund Hillary's Ocean to Sky Expedition in 1977 and the Saser Kangri III expedition in the Karakorams in 1986.